BEYOND DIAMOND RINGS

BEYOND DIAMOND RINGS

Kusum Choppra

 Cedar books

Published by:

Cedar books

An Imprint of
Pustak Mahal®, Delhi

J-3/16, Daryaganj, New Delhi-110002

☎ 23276539, 23272783, 23272784 • *Fax:* 011-23260518
E-mail: info@pustakmahal.com • *Website:* www.pustakmahal.com

Sales Centre

■ 10-B, Netaji Subhash Marg, Daryaganj, New Delhi-110002

☎ 23268292, 23268293, 23279900 • *Fax:* 011-23280567
E-mail: rapidexdelhi@indiatimes.com

■ **Hind Pustak Bhawan**
6686, Khari Baoli, Delhi-110006

☎ 23944314, 23911979

Branch Offices

Bengaluru: ☎ 22234025 • *Telefax:* 22240209
E-mail: pustak@airtelmail.in • pustak@sancharnet.in

Mumbai: ☎ 22010941
E-mail: rapidex@bom5.vsnl.net.in

Patna: ☎ 3294193 • *Telefax:* 0612-2302719
E-mail: rapidexptn@rediffmail.com

Hyderabad: *Telefax:* 040-24737290
E-mail: pustakmahalhyd@yahoo.co.in

© **Author**

ISBN 978-81-223-1089-4

Edition 2009

Printed at : Param Offsetters, Okhla, New Delhi-110020

Dedicated to

My mother, Ganga Khemlani
who wished to see her daughters make a name,
which I hope this book will do for me.
And
my family, Jogi, Gini, Mehirr, Jai Jai and Karrishma,
from whom I often 'stole' time to write this book.

ACKNOWLEDGEMENTS

Acknowledgements have to be many in a book with a canvas as large as this and characters so many.

First of all, I must acknowledge my debt to late Ms Edna Mahablesherwalla who helped me hone my writing skills to enable me to write this book.

Then there is a group of friends, whose encouragement and insightful feedback meant value addition to the various drafts of the manuscript to bring it to its present format. Those wonderful friends include Farida Wadia, who has always been an encouraging beacon in all the hardest of times, Usha Ram, my friend from my school days, now professor of psychology in the University of Pune, Sonal Kellog, a fellow journalist, Swati Medh and Rashminder Kaur, themselves busy writing; all of them took time off from their work to read and offer suggestions for further improvement.

My entire family deserves thanks for their patience while I remained preoccupied with writing. Most of all, I must mention the hard work my son Mehirr put in, doing everything to bring this book out on the stands. All I did was write it.

Finally the Cedar team, the Director Mr Rohit Gupta, and the editors Neha Gupta and Parul Jain, who did the most painstaking work of all, in the production of this book.

Many thanks to each one of you!

CONTENTS

INTRODUCTION

This is a novel set in the Bhaibund community, which is another of India's unfortunately diminishing communities; this one is shrunk not by under-development but by development, globalisation, migrations, intermarriages and a sad decimation of roots.

The Partition of India saw the total loss of Sindh to Pakistan.

Among the landed gentry, there were those who chose to stay back and those who came over to India, hoping it would be temporary. When it proved not, they were to forever ruminate over their losses. Rare were the landed Hindu Sindhis, who adjusted successfully to a new Post Partition life.

Among the educated and professional masses, for whom resettlement in India was comparatively less traumatic, there has been a gradual, almost imperceptible slipping into an Indian mould, which is secular or communal, but at the same time regionally impersonal until recently.

They adapted to the cities they settled in, they spoke the respective regional language and became almost sheepish about their *Sindhiyat*, especially the younger generation which often does not even speak the language.

Intermarriages and migrations too might have played a major role in the erosion of *Sindhiyat*. The Sindhi masses settled as trading communities in settlements, which evolved into dirty cesspools, once again deterring Generation X from acknowledging their Sindhi roots. Perhaps the only relief in this scenario was the spectacular commercial success of the Bhaibunds. For centuries, the Bhaibunds, the Merchant Princes of Sindh, have been the wanderers of the world, their caravans crisscrossing the globe, carrying marvels and conveniences from one end of the world to another.

Post Partition's major sociological development was a break with the ancient tradition of leaving Bhaibund families at home, while the menfolk lived and worked abroad, very often fathering a brood wherever they were. Genetically programmed almost, to live with minimal male interference in their day-to-day functioning, the homebound womenfolk blossomed on their own and took charge of their lives, making their menfolk almost incidental, as they lived abroad for long spells.

When they came home on long leaves, the women pussyfooted around them, knowing that their presence was perhaps a temporary intrusion.

Living together made for gender discomforts and often uninteresting subdued female characters, in sharp contrast to the flair for living displayed by lone women whose best was brought out by meek/absent husbands or widowhood.

Post Partition, families started to join the menfolk, living in Sindhi enclaves in virtually every capital and commercial city in the world, from Alaska to Zimbabwe. Up to a certain point, they clung to their *Sindhiyat*. Later came the impact of the ABCD (American Born Confused Desi) syndrome, which often clashed with their pronounced *Sindhiyat*. Confusions between the desires to merge where they lived and cross-border marriages also emerged, while accepting interesting customs of virtually every society they found themselves placed in. And, they made (and still make) flamboyant shows of their Sindhi roots, streaked with the colours of the world.

The novel tells the story of an extended family of women who came across in the Partition together and then went on to rehabilitate themselves in different parts of India and the globe, from Indonesia in the East to North Africa, and West Indies beyond.

1

MAYA

In many ways, it was a unique funeral. After a lifetime of being stifled, Maya had finally found a means of scoring, even if it was only in death. It was only right that Maya should have gone from the villa she was so proud and possessive of. I was glad she did leave from there.

Finally the long-closed, Big Door opened. They took the wasted dark body with the skin stretched tight over the thin bones and deep sunken eyes in huge sockets dominating the ravaged face.

Maya had lived a lifetime of pain, and had died without fulfilment. On the threshold of her life, she was unable to face the reality that she had desires left, which in turn could be desirable to anyone, even an electrician's errand boy, a strapping fellow, who was young enough to be her son.

Here were the ruins of a once proud woman, who withstood a lifetime of humiliation with the dignity of a queen, a Tragedy Queen. She perfectly resembled the part she played. Maya of the queenly grace, the lean tortured face, the undeveloped virgin breasts, slim figure, statuesque grace disguising her short height, a slight hesitant smile, long neck atop the narrow shoulders, thin arms and veined hands.

No one quite knew how she died. The young electrician was in a state of shock.

"I didn't do anything," he pleaded desperately.

They looked at her clothes which were in a complete disarray, the towel in her hand, and finally at the accused, "You must have done something to the electricity when she was in the bathroom."

The poor boy pointed at his bag.

"See, it's closed, I hadn't even opened my bag, when she collapsed."

No one noticed the disarray of his own clothes, the trousers barely held up by the belt-buckle, the shirt stuffed uneasily in, and the buttons askew.

I had my own ideas of how she died. Was it some romantic illusion?

After a lifetime of rejections, of being reminded of her rejection by her husband, told specifically in so many words and being made to realise it in so many ways, Maya's tired system couldn't deal with the fact that she was desirable, to anyone, even the electrician's boy.

Was Maya still pulling her robe together when she went to answer the doorbell? Did her robe slip open to reveal tempting glimpses of the unripened buds that had never felt the touch of a man? What crazed moment of desire had led the two to the sofa? Who led whom?

No one will ever know, but I was sure in my mind that Maya's tired heart collapsed in that moment, with the realisation that she was after all, desirable, to at least one man, even though he was ten years junior to her. The young man was so terrified by the thought that his careless tangling with a woman old enough to be his aunt, had led to her death that he fled and vanished.

To the family's astonishment, Maya's husband, Shyam flew down for her funeral. He had skipped the funeral of his beloved mother. But this time, he decided to come down.

Speaking to no one, he just spent the better part of a long hour staring down at the woman he had spurned. Death had smoothened her dark brow; her eyebrows almost rose as if asking a question.

Was that a hint of an ironic smile brightening the sad visage?

He saw the dead body before it was covered up. It was little more than skin and bones on a tiny frame. Did it make him wonder about the fabled queenly grace he had heard about for over three decades?

As he looked down at the dead woman, Shyam thought, "This woman... no, she is still a virgin, an unfulfilled virgin." He would have touched her, but he imagined that her dead mouth mocked at his outstretched hand. He pulled his hand back and turned to examine every inch of the house that Maya had built.

A massive tapestry of the Arab Sheikh making off with the Princess dominated the drawing room where she was laid out. He recognised it as one of the two he had sent down. Its twin adorned the drawing room of the Big House.

There were comfortable sofas around the walls of the oval room, punctuated by the doors opening into the generous balcony opening off the room. He walked out and entered the *puja* room at the end of the balcony. It was dominated by his mother's garlanded portrait and her beloved *Granth Sahib*.

Shyam turned back and through the narrow vestibule walked towards the bedrooms. The one nearest the back entrance was his mother's room, preserved, as it stood when she was alive, in pristine white. Only Ammi had never used the room. She had written to him, "Maya has made a nice bedroom for me, but what will I do in it alone? I prefer to spend my time on the *sandhal* (*divan*) outside where I can see what is going on."

Next to the unused white bedroom was the guestroom, the one renovated for his wife Rose when she had come. Rose had described it well – low twin beds pushed together under the fabulous *chikankari* bedcover, stained glass on the walls and matching night lamps that would turn the drapes to gold in their light.

The door to Maya's room was shut tight. As he pushed it open, Shyam sensed a flutter behind him. When she was alive, he had never met his dark wife. He had just seen her corpse. Now he was entering the bedroom that was so sacred to her that she allowed no one in, not even a servant.

She cleaned it herself. But someone had been there before him. The place had been rifled thoroughly, things stood askew, drawers with things spilling out, totally unlike the very meticulous Maya he had heard about.

It was a simple yet stately room, fully carpeted with rugs near the bed, the armoire and the desk with its numerous little drawers now spilling out. The table besides the bed held Maya's diaries.

Shyam flung open the massive armoire, row upon row of chiffon *saris*, all the hues of the palette and all manner of styles and designs were ranged there. A large drawer held Maya's collection of jewellery, comprising only pearl strings of all sizes, shades and styles, with simple studs or long matching earrings.

He stared. No one had told Shyam that Maya only wore pearls.

There was a knock at the door. His bhabhi, Sheel walked in hesitantly, offering a bunch of keys. Her hands shook as she pointed to a steel almirah in the corner and rushed out. The amount of cash in the little safe was much less than there should have been. Shyam could not find the heavy sets of diamonds and emeralds, which he had brought for his marriage forty years ago, five years before the Partition. He wondered what else was missing, as he casually pocketed the keys and sat on the bed.

Shyam was not quite sure of his feelings. Was it relief or guilt? Or both?

It was her funeral which had drawn me here, to promptly anoint the place, the city of crones – all of them togged in the most sophisticated whites, painted and plumed, perfumed and ornamented. Only the white and the absence of any (but the faintest of) lipsticks indicated that it was a funeral, not a *kirtan*, kitty or a kocktail party.

There was something macabre about the crones, as they congregated there with their vacant eyes and white glitzy costumes. Their feet were elegantly well-kept, polished and well-rounded. The arms were neatly waxed and fingernails painted, casually or otherwise. The fingers were often twisted but flickered with diamond rings. The faces resembled well-blushed steamed cabbages. The hair was clipped and dyed to an elegance that belied the narrow minds.

Blank desires, with few interests other than food, movies and clothes, blindly aping the western style or those of film stars in the latest movie, rarely realising that what they aped from the West was often the baseness, and not the best of the West. Food was a passion, social commitments a compulsion, *satsangs* a pastime, a personal guru, the latest status symbol.

With all the money they collectively represented, one could genuinely expect better surroundings, but the little congregation settled happily enough on the threadbare duresses, surrounded by the peeling walls, slightly faded fake flowers and curtains, the ubiquitous gaudy cover to the *Granth Sahib*, edged with the twisted tassels which added nothing to it.

Many of the crones were daughters of the family. An odd *bahu* or two hardly made any difference to the weight of the daughters who dominated the little community. They looked after the elderly parents.

Still considered a liability and a curse, but strangely, at last the daughters were really sought after. Of course, if she was divorced, or widowed, it was better. The burden of guilt was smaller for giving her a home to fall back on, rather than keeping her unmarried. 'The *punya* of *kanyadaan* and all that jazz...'

No, the daughters were not prized for their money or earnings.

Not at all – there was plenty to go about, even with the unending avarice.

Rather it was the need for a caretaker of an old age, held captive by the bonds of filial relations, which the sons had long since broken, and by their own unfulfilled suppressed desires – manifested in the cussed warpedness of their fingers, toes, the torso, of their mind and the heart, in their glassy eyes and the chill scolding tones, sweet perfumes and henna notwithstanding.

After a while, it was no longer the battle of the bulge, which was important. The proliferation of various dieticians, the ubiquitous gyms and the walking paths helped the crones win that one.

It was the battle against age that took precedence, the battles against wrinkles, the greying hair, the sagging cheeks which became the focus of life with an array of weapons against the advancing age, with the help of the creams, the hair dyes and the yet to come Botox treatment that took care of the look.

But what about the mindset which even the personal gurus could not help? That fear of being old and the frenzied obsession to remain young, as if Old Age was a disease as dangerous as AIDS, to be fought off at all costs.

Everyone reared back at the word old, "How can you say that I am old? If somebody says that to you, how will you feel?? I am a mature person not old. Who says I am old... my Guruji says... blah, blah, blah."

The battle against age and the personal guru were the latest preoccupations of the successor crones.

"My Guruji says, you can wear what you like. All that matters is that your thoughts should be pure. So I don't wear white all the time like them."

Other Gurujis prescribed weekly or fortnightly *satsangs*, with a community get-together, annual visits to far off *ashrams*, a prescribed dress code or a prayer code or a meal code or whatever. The point was to prove that "My Guruji Bestest…" just like that advertisement of "My Papa Bestest". They offered solace to those who had lagged behind in the race, who were reduced to virtual irrelevance in a world dominated by cash and finance, big and bigger diamonds, fancy and fancier homes, giant and gigantic business houses... and of course, the biggest ego trip of them all was a jet setting life abroad. Those left at home, needed a shoulder to lean on, although nowadays, wandering Gurujis were also huge in demand, crossing the seven seas to cater to the needs of their flock, scattered across the globe.

Personality battles and issues, which were the flavour of life, included conveniently dictated marriages, which were still the order of the day. Such marriages ensured stability, an acceptance of societal norms – no high passions in marriage, no dramatic gut-wrenching lows either. Such placidity was broken by the inquisitiveness of the people who were interested in knowing who married whom and why, how much dowry was given, who was invited, etc.

Instead of the obsession with husbands and lovers, there were the women-centric events, lunches and teas, rather than dinners, *satsangs*, kitties and plain gossip sessions, engagements, long drawn out weddings, birthdays, naming and *janiyas*, the *pujas* and *kathas* and the fasts, at all of which male presence was token at best.

Thus the men were a superfluous presence. Almost unwanted. In any case, there were a bare handful, all with prosperous bellies tucked into expensive imported silk shirts. Everything was imported, from the *banians* peeping through, to the socks, shoes and handkerchiefs and the lavish after-shave.

They had laid Maya out in grandeur. The Big Door, locked for almost a quarter of a century since Maya's house was built, was finally opened for the first and the last time to take Maya out of her house. It was the only time that anyone could remember the door standing open – to receive streams of mourning relatives.

That Big Door had been the sign of Maya's extravagance and her rebellion. When the House was being built, the family had sat down to allot the space. It was Ammi, Maya's mother-in-law who ruled then.

"Maya and I will live upstairs," she said.

They were the Queens of the Mansion. The big drawing room, the puja room and the guestroom were to be upstairs. Gunwant, Ammi's younger son, and his family would live downstairs with the comatose Bharti.

There was a staircase at the back of the house, but the main entrance had a handsome teak polished door in the front, which opened into a tiny vestibule downstairs, with the drawing room on the left and the bedrooms on the right. No one knew why Maya allowed the builder to make it that way.

From the vestibule, rose a beautiful, tightly curled staircase. Once the House was ready, the old lady decreed, "We will use the back stairs. This Front Door will remain closed until Shyam comes home. Only then will it be opened."

The Big Door had never been opened all these years. It was prepared when Shyam wrote about his trip with his new wife, but the trip did not happen. When his wife Rose came alone, Maya decided to receive her at the back entrance. The only time Shyam came, it was a surprise and a surreptitious visit. He sprinted up the back stairs in the dark, so no one would know he came.

A sturdy grill was put into place in front of the Big Door. The grill was held in place by a massive lock and the back entrances serviced both upstairs and downstairs. The downstairs residents balked, but Maya quite liked using the back stairs. As she went up and down, or even stood at her landing, she was in her own little world.

Behind the house, at the end of a short driveway was the garage, with the servants' quarters on top; her collection of pots hedged the small paved back courtyard, and beyond it was a tiny Japanese garden, complete with a miniscule bridge over an often empty pond, a minute stone bench and a pocket handkerchief sized lawn, with one solitary badam tree, single and majestic, despite its lack of height; rather its umbrella made up for that to give it a standalone space.

At one time of the year, the effervescent green of the new leaves was ushered in by one last glorious burst of ochre by the older leaves – Was it the sign of the old order being passed on to the new?

Ranged in tiered umbrellas graded in size – largest, larger, large, small, smaller and smallest at the top – all of these would float lazily down to earth at pre-determined intervals, carpeting the dry, moist earth with a crackling carpet on which cats, mice and kids could tumble with equal glee. But they never did.

The garden was Maya's indulgence. It was a source of a secret as well as obvious pleasure to her. No one saw her going there too frequently, in fact, hardly at all. She used to gaze at it from her landing only. Was she seeing herself in those foreign parts that she alone in the family could never visit?

There was a high wall to keep the prying eyes away from the house. Standing atop her stairs, Maya could peer into the neighbours' houses to see their everyday lives and thereby realising what she missed out in her life. She stubbornly adhered to her extravagant fancy against the loud, raucous, mercenary assaults of the family.

"Such a waste of space! What is the use of this silly garden? We can easily make rooms and rent them out," argued Gunwant's wife, hopelessly, knowing fully well that with Ammi backing her, Maya would carry the day, since Shyam had left all matters in their hands.

No one could quite remember when and how Maya took control of the family.

At first, the family revolved around Ammi, who brought Maya home as Shyam's bride, who soothed her desperate tears on that traumatic wedding night when Shyam had walked out in a huff immediately after lifting her *ghunghat*.

"Couldn't you find someone darker and uglier for me?" he threw at his mother, as he walked out from the house, with no inclinations to return.

Later, Ammi got Shyam tracked down, rebuked him for the tragedy his thoughtlessness had wrecked on Maya and extracted the promise of a lifelong commitment. Shyam gave the promise with a proviso of his own, "Yes, Maya is my wife, I married her, but I will not live with her. I will do what I want with my life, but I shall support her to the best of my abilities."

The old lady had shown the letter to all to consolidate Maya's position and support her own selection of a dark but wealthy *bahu*.

The War intervened and everything went haywire. For several months, no money came through and the old lady was forced to plunge into her savings. There was no word from either of her sons. But she was not alone. The entire community of women was in severe trouble as all the lines of communication were broken. That is when the community spirit triumphed, when every household aided the other to tide over the crises.

This was the community that had, for centuries, sent its men out all over the globe to trade. Trading was not only in their blood, but it had seeped into their marrow. No young man considered himself even half a man, if he had not earned his fortune in business in some foreign corner of the world.

The women lived at home, upholding family and traditional values, against all the new ideas that the men were exposed to in their foreign travels, disciplining themselves and the families in the absence of all, barring the oldest of the retired men. Wives saw their husbands once in two-three years, if they were lucky. Children saw their fathers only after having reached the age of two or more. And similar intervals thereafter, the boys used to count the days until they could also take off for foreign parts. The family ties became weak as mothers could only see their sons after decades on end. Most however, did return after every two-three years for a well-earned vacation with the family, to make renewed acquaintance with their wives and children, living in their elaborate homes, full of global knickknacks brought home by the men to Hyderabad Sindh, inviting the envy of many other Sindhis, both the Muslim Sindhis and the non Bhaibund Sindhis.

Of course, whichever of the men came back, spoke of fabulous business being done all over the world, which included South Africa, Gibraltar, Eden, Singapore, Japan, Philippines etc, wherever the trading community flourished with the militaries devouring stores in bulk. Whosoever arrived, came laden with gold and cash as a courier for dozens of households. In no time at all, accounts were settled to pave the way for fresh lending and careful borrowing, until the next courier came.

During the period of the War, Shyam dropped out of sight. With no inflow of money, the aunts and the cousins had a field day in making life miserable for the abandoned bride. They would make taunting remarks by calling her 'The Black Bride'.

No one knew anything about Shyam's wartime adventures. He came back after the War was over and the talk of Partition had already risen to a crescendo. No one quite believed that talk.

"It'll blow away," they thought. Stories came through of people leaving Karachi for Bombay with their families, even from Shikaarpur and Multan. Here, in Hyderabad, the women remained watchful in their own enclaves, as none of the men were available to organise any move. By the time the letters came through, ordering them to go, it was rather late.

Partition was already beginning to scorch the land. The older and bolder women got together for a conference. Should they all go together or in small groups? Which would be more dangerous? There was much talk of loot and rape. Who would protect the younger women and the little girls? What to take? How much? How to leave the rest?

Like the others, Ammi was quite frantic for her sons.

Why was she never that concerned about Baba? One never knew.

Ammi had sent word to Gunwant to track down Shyam. When Shyam's letter finally arrived, long after the Partition, Ammi celebrated with a *satya narayan katha* in the Big House, which was the sanctuary of the family in post partition India.

It had been acquired long ago when one of Amma's sons fell under Gandhiji's spell and set up a Khadi business here. After the flight from Pakistan, the Big House oversaw the settling across the globe of the extended family, mostly Amma's five surviving sons and innumerable daughters, Ammi's two sons and the offspring of various uncles and cousins.

For Ammi, Shyam's letter with good news was a personal triumph. Shyam was true to his word. He had made good money in the War and sent lavish amounts home.

"Build a big new home," he said, "for both your *bahus*."

He took Gunwant under his wing and called up a steady stream of cousins to work in his various enterprises and those of his associates. They then sent a regular flow of money to resettle the extended family after the wrench of Partition.

Shyam sent everything, goods and cash to take care of his mother. Over the years, Ammi leaned on Maya to participate in the decisions, before finally leaving it all to her, overriding even Gunwant. It was this that caused endless heartburn and resentment, especially to Gunwant's pretty wife Sheel.

It became even worse when Shyam decreed that one of the men of the family should remain at home. After Gunwant met with a debilitating accident, he sent him back. The money to set up a shop at home came via Ammi and Maya, but Gunwant had no business skills. His frequent losses were covered from Maya's drafts, at which Sheel's resentments brewed.

Another resentment earlier was the task allotted to her after Maya's villa was built, which included the care of the comatose Bharti. Few remembered Bharti. Sheel, who got married long after the Partition, had never seen her in her heyday. Everyone said that she had been a beauty with a sharp tongue to keep her bhabhis in check.

Now she was a sorry mass, laid out on a string bed, someone who had to be taken care of. She was avoided even by servants, unless they were strictly supervised. It required bathing to keep her clean, oiling to keep her skin soft, exercises to keep her muscles supple, liquid feeds and turning over to prevent bedsores.

It was not a pretty sight at all and Bharti ended up occupying one corner of the backroom, quite neglected, except by the maid whose family depended on the services she rendered to Bharti.

I often wondered whether Shyam ever felt guilty about Maya.

He was otherwise quite a sensitive person. He looked after his extended family and had taken care to give his slighted wife an edge over others in society, which included a massive bungalow of her own, with his own brother almost dependent on her largesse. After Ammi, all of Shyam's money to his relatives flowed through Maya's ledgers. If he sent some extra money to others unofficially, then no one spoke of it.

Shyam never spoke of Maya to anyone who visited him. His only communication was with Ammi. After she died, his office dealt with the financial matters and his letters were addressed to Sheel whom he had met when she had flown out for a short holiday, which had left her dizzy with exuberance. It was the only time in her life when she was on top of Maya.

The guilt was all of his Ammi's doing, constantly reminding him that he had ruined Maya's life and that he owed her. He often talked about it to his wife Rose, but nothing that she ever said had relieved him of that feeling of guilt.

The present feeling of relief was the natural fallout of that guilt. It came because of the lifting of that yoke of guilt; relief that he need no longer feel guilty about Maya's aborted life. Not that Maya had ever said anything to him.

After that dramatic exit from the bridal chamber, they neither met nor spoke to each other. All their communication was through Ammi and the letters. The only time in all these years that Shyam had come to India was after the trips of his second wife, Rose and his children. He had told his mother to make sure that Maya was not there and the old woman, torn between her duty to her wronged *bahu* and her long lost son, had arranged for Maya to go away.

Shyam's trip was a well-kept secret. Ammi had gone to the Big House to plot with Dadi.

"Shall I suggest a trip to Bombay? No. Bangalore? Hyderabad? Ajmer? Haridwar-Badrinath yatra?" Dadi had other plans.

"Ammi, I will take care of it."

Dadi popped in to see Maya and almost begged of her.

"Maya, please, I'll never go alone, but I need to go to this *baba*. He alone can cure me. With you, I'll feel safe too. You can face off anyone who tries to act funny."

Ammi added her entreaties and Maya agreed. How could she otherwise? Both of them were her two main allies. The thought of betrayal by them never occurred to her.

It was with an immense sense of responsibility that Maya set off with Dadi. "One never know these days. Even these *babas* and *sants* could be villains, taking advantage of single women," she pronounced undauntedly.

Their guide, Dadi's servant, Gangubai took offence at such a blasphemous talk.

"How can you say such a thing? This *baba* has wrought so many miracles, Mayabai, you have no idea. We live in the city, with doctors and hospitals. In the village, where will women go? These *mard log* spend money on themselves. Even if a buffalo falls ill, they will spend money to bring it to the city. But what about the woman? Who spends money on her medicine? Rather let her be as she is or let her die and bring another younger one, which means more dowry and more variety."

Gangubai could have bit her tongue. Why did she have to say all that? She also knew Maya's story but now didn't know how to retract. She pushed on.

"It happens all the time. Ammibai is very good and so is *sahib* – they have given you everything, house, clothes, money, status – everyone is not like them," she ended weakly, adding that her own daughter had come back home and eked out a living by massaging new born babies and bringing their obese mothers back into shape.

Perhaps Maya was high on her first outing in what seemed a lifetime. She was breathing deeply as they trekked from the bus stop in the village, through the fields and trees, towards the *baba's ashram*, deep in the jungle on the foothills.

That year summer had an unusual flavour, under the dusty heat there was a distinct chill. In any case, summer's early mornings and late nights are pleasantly cool. But now they were chilly. Even the day had an underlying foreboding chill. Was it a premonition of an impending disaster or some mishap? What was it?

Maya looked all around her with fascination, taking in the checkered view of the fields at the bottom of the hill, the neatly thatched houses, which looked dark but probably cool from inside, despite the heat outside, the scraggly children, the variegated greens of the undergrowth and the dappled patches of sunlight filtering through the trees overhead. She was so engrossed by her first sights of the variety of the butterflies and the squirrels that she barely heard Gangubai's monologue.

Maya would never have dreamt that at this very moment, Shyam was leaping up the steps of her house to meet his mother. The old woman hugged him close to feel him against her chest, as she could not see his face with tear clouded eyes. It was an uneasy meeting for both the mother and the son.

"I met your children and Rose. Maya also met them. Even Rose met Maya. Why are you still afraid of meeting her?"

"I am not afraid," the response was a bit too quick, "I just want you to remain with me only." Shyam was unable to explain or to justify his insistence on Maya's absence while he met his mother.

Both spoke quickly, as if wanting to get things off their chest as quickly as possible before Maya came home, knowing fully well that she would only return the next evening, and by that time, Shyam would have left.

For obvious reasons, Ammi had told no one about Shyam's visit except Dadi. She had earlier even debated with Dadi.

"I can't send Gunwant's wife away as Maya is to go. Besides, if Sheel opens her mouth, Maya will be hurt."

The old woman tried another trick. She decreed that the drawing room downstairs needed a proper spring-clean and threatened to come down to do it herself. This kept Sheel busy enough not to watch the gate.

Ammi spent the day gazing at her son and Shyam in worshipping her. Both hardly ate any of the dishes that Ammi had ordered for him. It was this that gave the game away... much later.

Servants began to gossip and the cook upstairs mentioned the special guest who didn't eat, to the cook downstairs, who mentioned it to Sheel, who asked Maya, who asked Ammi, who tried to pretend ignorance.

"When have I kept track of who eats how much? And since when have you indulged in the gossip of the menials?"

But it rankled. Maya even peeked into the guestroom. It was undisturbed. Did it mean that a guest was sleeping in the drawing room? Impossible. Who can that be?

The mystery remained as unresolved as her trip with Dadi. They had reached the *ashram* quite exhausted. After a refreshing meal and rest, they entered the *baba's* sanctum.

His piercing eyes read their faces thoroughly. Gangubai remained respectfully outside. Maya met his eyes boldly and felt him looking her over. He said, "Go, child, you are troubled, but it is in your Fate. Learn to accept it and find peace in it...." Some such prattle, which gave no solution to her daily dilemmas.

Dadi was escorted by a group of women for her treatment.

"*Baiji aap chalo. Nahi, aap nahi....*" Maya was disappointed when she was not allowed to be present. When the older woman came back much later, she was tired and sleepy. Hot milk, infused with herbs, awaited her. After a sound night's sleep, Dadi awoke to an unusual mellowness, unnatural for the severity, which one expected from her.

"What did he do?"

Dadi busied herself with nothing and turned away.

"Nothing, I don't know what it was. They applied some medicine and it burnt like hell, so it was allowed to cool down. Now it feels much better…."

Dadi was obviously being evasive, but Maya too was not quite herself. Maybe it was the strange setting. It was not till weeks later, that she started wondering about the hot medicine which needed cooling with whatever was painted on Dadi's lower torso and upper legs, till her uncharacteristic mellow mood wore off and the usual severity surfaced.

Seeking explanations only brought on sorrow. Dadi was an expert at deflecting.

"What do you mean, what did the *baba* do? Do we know what the doctors do with us? At least this treatment gives me relief for almost a year at least. And it got you away from here."

"Away from here? Why?" Maya sputtered.

For once Dadi was caught without a convenient answer. She was forced to confess. But if she expected Maya to confront Ammi, she was wrong. Maya swallowed Shyam's visit, with her queenly act, mulling over it and digested it without a word to anyone, not even Ammi.

"What right have I to object?" she mulled.

But she felt her house had been violated. It took her a long time to get over the fact that Shyam came in her absence and looked over the house. An almost savage spring-clean astounded everyone, it was if she was shaking Shyam's dust off her house.

Everything was shuffled, even the pictures. She had no idea that he was so engrossed in his mother that he barely noticed his surroundings; except the white room where he had curled at his mother's feet late in the night.

He remained out of sight there, when Sheel had popped up for an hour 'to give the old lady company in Maya's absence'. The old lady shooed her out, asking for some more dinner as she was hungry, but that extra helping went unheeded and caused a lot of questions later.

*****

2

MAYA-THE VISITS

L ater, Maya was almost relieved that she did not know of Shyam's visit until it was over. She could recall the terror and tension of the earlier two visits of Shyam's wife, Rose and his children in chilling graphic detail.

Years ago, Shyam had written to say that his teenage daughters would be coming to India, on their world tour. They wanted to meet their grandma and Indian relatives.

"Look after them, for my sake," said the letter, perhaps fearing that Ammi may not accept her grandchildren born of a foreign mother whom she had neither seen nor selected.

The letter also had another strange intonation. Instead of pleading for Ammi's love, it demanded, as if Shyam knew he was putting both Ammi and Maya to test. The letter said that his children were mature now and wanted to learn about their father's background, to see the places where he had spent his youth. He had organised a tour that would also take them to Hyderabad, Sindh (now in Pakistan), where he was born and grew up, along with the extended family here. Extra funds were remitted to take care of the extra expenses on the visit.

The old lady showed the letter to Maya rather hesitatingly. She knew it would hurt. Shyam had written that he expected that "everyone will treat my children as the children of the family, as they rightly deserve to be." This last piece flew out of the carefully tinted paper and went straight into Maya's heart.

"He's talking to me," she said with some agitation, as her placid life swirled about her. Despite her peculiar situation as an 'Abandoned Woman', thanks to Ammi, she had been able to arrange her life admirably. She was accepted by the whole of the extended family, was invited and entertained everywhere, if she would let them.

She wore the best of clothes, the most sophisticated jewellery and accessories, the latest transport, with first her own buggy, then a rickshaw of her own and later a car, among the first in the family. She had a house of her own, which rivalled the Big House, architecturally and importance wise, with Maya Queen Bee residing there.

Now she had to pay for that Queen Bee status. Years of her Queen Bee status had given her a queenly grace with traces of arrogance, which visibly got drained out of her face when the import of the letter sank in. These were Shyam's children from his second wife, Rose. They were grownup girls. The letter made no mention of how much they knew of his background and his relationships. Everyone would be easy to explain, mother, brother, bhabhi, sisters, masi, chachi, and cousins.... But what about Maya? His first wife?

The face she presented to Ammi was impassive.

"I'll get the guestroom spring-cleaned," she said. In the stillness of her mind, Maya saw alternate scenarios, scores of them flashed by as she struggled to decide on a line of action – how to cope with this? What was this? A threat?

Whatever it was, it loomed large ahead of her. Time was at a premium, less than a week to organise the entire schedule, buy that car, and make reservations everywhere. Who would escort them? Whom should she trust?

Maya held an informal conference. She knew that the oldest of
her generation, Sundri came to the Big House every Friday for
her weekly visit. Others also dropped in and it became quite a
gathering. Maya ordered her rickshaw out and went to the *bazaar*
to enquire about the status of her car application and its tentative
release.

Those were the days when one waited years for a car to come
from the official quota and paid money under the table to get the
matter expedited by a few months.

"*Jaldi karo, mehmaan aane wale hai,*" she commanded, "Phone
them and tell them it is urgent now."

She picked up Ammi's weekly medicines. Today she did not dally
in any shop.

She was off to the Big House. "*Khandar batate hain ki imarat
haseen rahi hogi.*" (The ruins indicate that it must have been
grand once).

The massive multi-storied house stood at the bottom of its own
sizeable cul-de-sac. Shorn now of its outer grandeur, its imposing
gentility was surrounded by the modern shabbiness of kiosks, larris
and shops. The wooden gate was tumbling down and the massive
iron gates long torn out of their posts.

The lawn was non-existent, the lone garage looked shabby without
its *ghari*, the *ghariwan's* quarters now housed families of former
servitors, the *dhobi's* son graduated to a 'drycleaner', the '*nai*' to
a 'hairdresser', the '*darzi*' to a 'boutique', even a beauty parlour
into a day care centre-cum-crèche. The short lane was inhabited by
more decrepit remnants of the past grandeur, an old-style *halwai*, a
grocer, a *pansari*, a baker and other assorted services.

Once upon a time, this *haveli* had been a hub, surrounded by the
elegant homes of relatives and hangers-on. Now it had been pushed
to the sidelines by the ubiquitous modern housing and shopping
complexes surrounding the suburban clubs. Not that anyone really

paid attention. There was an inverted snobbery in going against the migration to new fancy complexes. "So nouveau riche, *chhi!*"

"I was just passing by," said Maya but no one was deceived. In fact, they had been discussing the trip themselves. How Shyam had thought of sending his children home after so long? Was this the prelude to his coming back home after all? With or without his family? What would now happen to Maya? Would he keep Maya or chuck her out? What will happen to the Queen Bee?

The shrill, catty voices had clashed with the more compassionate ones. The younger ones, the good-looking ones did not have that fear, but amongst the older women, Maya's pinched face and unripe body was a constant reminder of their own good luck. They surrounded her.

"What preparations have you made?"

Maya took a deep breath as she searched the circle around her, organising her thoughts. "Nothing yet. News travel fast, the letter came only this morning," her lips curled in their familiar ironic twist. Sheel had been busy, spreading the news.

Dadi stood up. Taking Maya by her arm, she led her inside, to her own sanctum. Sundri, Bhagwanti, Pushpa and Parvati Bhabhi followed. The rest of the younger crowd knew they were out of it and quickly dispersed.

"Maya, what have you thought?"

"All of you, you tell me. What should I do? My heart is broken again. After all these years, is he trying to test me? What does he mean 'treat them as children of the family as they rightly deserve to be'? Would they have been treated otherwise? Have I ever slipped up in giving anyone due respect, or even undue respect? How much all of you raged over allowing Jaideep and Latu to set up a house and a shop separately? They didn't want to live with us or with Sheel. I backed them, even before Shyam did." Then she reeled off the list of family rebels, whose cause she had pleaded admirably in the past.

"How could he insult me so?" she ended almost piteously, her queenly dignity in shambles around her.

The sight was not a pretty one and the others were quite taken aback. But Maya recovered before them.

"I'll teach him a lesson. I won't entertain them. Book them into a hotel and I'll go away…"

Suddenly tears poured down her cheeks. Wearily she rested her head on Dadi's shoulders. The older woman put an arm around Maya and let her weep it out. Gently she patted her till she calmed down.

"Now, listen, Maya, we all have to face reality. And reality is that Shyam is now, for the first time in so many years, demanding his pound of flesh."

Maya began to object, but Dadi was inexorable.

"Listen to me, he has, against all the odds and the vicious advice of many, supported you all through these years. Yes, he was never physically there with you, but he had provided the best of everything for you including a house with the servants. Now all he is asking is that his children get to see his house, his mother and relatives, to get to know their Sindhi background. Is that too much to ask? They are children of a foreign woman who have been born and brought up abroad. Should they not learn about their father's background? His society? His family?

"Now, suppose Shyam was here and he had brought another woman, whom you had to face every day? To see her children grow up in front of you? Face them at every family function? How many could you have avoided? Eventually they would be in your face every day, every week, all the time. This is once in a lifetime, three or four days to pay for years of peace and comfort. Is it too big a price to pay?" Dadi paused for a breath. Maya's face dropped down.

"Let me go away for some time," she said.

"Where will you go? Have your parents ever raised a voice about Shyam in all these years? Will they back you now? Your sister lives in town. How will it look if the children come and there is no one at home to look after them and you are at your sister's place? She will attend the lunch party since her husband works for Shyam. She'll come, and you'll sit at home? Maya, don't tempt Fate. Don't challenge your Luck. If Shyam loses his head (there came that all-too-familiar threat), he may even stop the money he's sending. And where will you be then?"

All her life, Maya had been governed by that threat, that invisible Damocles' Sword hanging over her queenly head – of Shyam's goodwill and its withdrawal. All this despite his pointed ignorance of her existence altogether. This threat was the steel claw inside the velvet glove of the otherwise gentle, affectionate relationship with her mother-in-law. Any time Maya seemed to be slipping off the beaten path, or asserting herself, it was 'what if Shyam…'.

Now, it was impossible to counter that inexorable logic.

"Maya, there is no one to turn to, who will not be intimidated by the power of Shyam's wealth. Remember, he is not the only one who has made millions, others have done so too. But no one has spread out those millions into so many within the extended family, provided so much employment and business opportunities to improve the lot of so many families as Shyam has."

All the while, Shyam used his mother and through her, Maya, as the conduit for the help and the largesse, thereby creating for Maya, the title of the Queen Bee in the little community. Too many people, including many from her own family were too personally indebted to Shyam to countenance any revolt by Maya against his wishes. She was the proverbial spider trapped in her own silken web woven out of Shyam's golden drafts.

"And what has he asked for? Only that his children be given a befitting status, one that they deserve anyway as his children. He is your husband, woman. His children are your children. Look at it that way," chipped in Didi, severely tempted to shake the 'silly woman'.

But Maya seemed quite inconsolable. This was a shattering blow to her pride, which was the only thing that shored up her barren life. She had lulled herself into a careful acceptance of her situation as an abandoned woman. Damn it... that is what she was after all. She always avoided delicate situations such as interacting with the newly weds, the new born babies, the numerous ceremonies connected with them. She was gracious in sending gifts, but often absented herself from such occasions.

Maya rarely attended weddings either. Whenever it took place in the family, and it was quite often in such a large one that she would shut herself up in her eerie, aloof, cold, dry-eyed and distant room. She and Ammi would decide how much to give, but only Ammi and Sheel would go. Maya would put in an appearance at the grand finale, the reception, only if it was for a very close relative with whom she shared some personal bond. Same was with children's births and birthday parties. But yes, she was very much there at all funerals or whenever someone fell ill, always as the Queen Bee, the Lady Bountiful. Now this?

Slowly the inexorable arguments began to make an impact. Maya's restless breathing quieted. And even as the Dadis carried on, her mind began to function. Suddenly she stood up, wiping her face.

"I must plan everything," she announced as she left abruptly, leaving the Dadis looking at each other. What was she going to plan? The visit? Some ugly incident? A disaster?

In the ultimate analysis, Maya realised, it was Ammi, not Shyam, she needed to take recourse to. Ammi was her key to Shyam. She needed Ammi beside her to face up to Shyam.

One look at Maya's face and Ammi said, "I know what you are going through. But I know you are my good girl. Now stop fulminating against it and let's decide what is to be done. Have you thought about it?"

Maya nodded. She just asked one question.

"Do they know me?" Ammi's eyes were as hopeless as hers.

"I don't know." She held up her hand to stop Maya's opening lips. "And I am not going to ask. Take it from there." Maya swallowed, paused and then squaring her thin shoulders visibly, unveiled the nebulous shape of her plan.

Gunwant received the girls at the international airport and brought them home in an inter-city taxi. There, at the gate, they were received by Ammi and Sheel, grandma and aunt leading an excited horde of other aunts and cousins.

As they climbed the stairs, Maya and the Dadis welcomed them into the house. The girls knew Dadi and Sheel from their visits to their home. The familiar faces were a welcome island in the sea of strangers, whom they could only get to know gradually. Neither their word nor their deed gave away their inevitable suspense over the identity of the frail dark elegant lady, who did not introduce herself.

Maya had drawn up a busy itinerary for the 'tourists', roping in some of the younger people to escort the girls. She found herself reluctant to utter the words 'Shyam's daughters'.

Reshma and Ruth were a lovely pair; their bright eager faces took in their grandma and recognised Gunwant, Sheel and Dadi from their trips to their home. They met everyone and wondered at the dark, graceful woman, who was obviously the hostess, who had not introduced herself, nor was she introduced by anyone. Ruth caught herself staring at the carefully placid visage, the deep sorrowful eyes, wondering 'Who is she? She even has her own room here'.

But it would seem rude to ask. By keeping everyone busy throughout the lunch and the tea, Maya avoided any direct interaction with the girls beyond the basic civilities. She had in any case, after making all the preparations, abdicated the direct guest hospitality to Sheel.

"You know the girls, they will obviously feel more comfortable with you," she entreated. Sheel was flattered into accepting Maya's request.

In the evening, a gaggle of cousins bore Reshma and Ruth off to youthful pursuits. They had much to discuss – college, discos, freedom or the lack of it, fashion, pocket money, music, so much more...

Those were the days when the strongly starched middle class Maharashtrian flavour of the Jungli Maharaj Road had just been infiltrated by the Madrasi cafes, *idli-dosas* and *sambhar-wada* flavours, not yet the pizzas and the burgers. The cousins wanted to show off to Ruth and Reshma what their city had to offer.

The approach to the watering hole that was the latest flavour of the month was quite un-prepossessing. One barely avoided slipping into a narrow gutter-ditch to reach the parking lot. There matters improved.

Entering a small white wicket gate in a true-blue American 'estyle', one stepped onto a flagged path leading to a club house-style structure, passing through what seemed to be a well laid out garden, lit by the garish coloured lights. The scene was quite obviously reminiscent of the scenes in the Hindi films of the '60s, in which the hero and heroine sang a song gamboling in such illuminated gardens with fountains throwing up their liquid music in the background. Only here the fountains were missing.

Instead, the inside boasted of a proper, old-style jukebox, 'specially imported' from the United States, in an Indian counterpart of the infamous Potel, which was the name given to the motels run by the Gujarati Patels. While one brother decorated his motel in the

US of A to dazzle his American clientele with ethnic artefacts, the rejected décor of the motel was sent to dazzle the local tourists in India. It was considered to be a fair exchange.

Maya counted the hours, every now and then checking out the gaily-decorated guestroom, decorated with posters and teddies, to make sure that nothing was missing. The room was next to her own, so she knew exactly when they came in, exhausted after a long day, full of seeing new faces and new places. Did they know who she was?

The visit went like a clockwork. Thankfully, it was a short one – four days full of visiting relatives. Reshma and Ruth were totally overawed by the Big House. Entering through the nondescript entrance and rather worn out stone steps at the road entrance, they gasped at the grandeur of the broad staircase with its enormous, arched stained glass window which bound up one side of the staircase, just like the ones in the churches of yore, except that instead of Jesus and Mary, there were flowers and abstract figures.

The enormous drawing room, populated by comfortable old sofas was dominated by a massive woven tapestry on one wall, depicting a handsome Arabian Sheikh and his men carrying off the Princess, with the inhabitants of the fort twirling their swords in hot pursuit, in vivid reds and elegant Prussian blues. It was the twin of the one in Maya's house and lit up with a Bohemian crystal chandelier.

The heavy mahogany dining table, with the lions' claw legs and delicately embroidered table cloth had matching armoires, loaded with china and crystal from the Far East and the West. Along with it, there were entire services of Sledge ware and Limoges, Chinese dragons, delicate gold-edged roses from Japan and modern geometrics and figurines jostled for space with soup tureens and sauceboats, amidst elaborately framed photographs of handsome couples, dumpled and dimpled darlings in the exotic global locales.

To the left was the bar, with its top boasting of slithers of gold veined marble. The front panel was make-believe of an ancient pirate's trunk, complete with the brass accessories, so reminiscent of pictures of Long John Silver's 'Yo Ho Ho and a bottle of rum'. Four revolving stools stood in front, the mirror and the glass shelves showed off a remarkable collection of crystal and liquor.

Yet, the signs of wear and tear were obvious all over the house, reflected in the worn patches in the carpets underfoot and discreet patches in the tapestries and the curtains. Here was no ostentatious preservation of the family antiques and the silver. Rather it was an almost casual neglect, which extended into the bedrooms still boasting of ubiquitous steel almirahs, the status symbols of a bygone era, alongside the modern armoires.

They peeped into the spacious airy kitchen with a split personality – Ours and Theirs.

Theirs had a four door fridge-cum-freezer, a juicer and a host of other gizmos from foreign parts. What it did not have was a sink. None of the foreign-based bhabhis would soil their hands washing up back home, when there were any number of *bais* to do the job for them.

So the massive ancient stone sink was spruced up with a stainless steel drain board under the traditional wire basket in the Our side of the kitchen, with its four ring gas hotplate, a totally functional *chulha* for the daily quota of roasted papad which only tasted right when done on a *chulha*, rather than on a gas ring, and of course the slow cooked *handi* mutton.

There was a commodious fridge, toaster, mixie, the pressure cookers and *dekchis* of all shapes and sizes, proclaiming their antiquity. Leading them off was a stone shelved store room, populated by storage bins of all sizes, earthen jars with the stocks of pickles and provisions.

Although the house had only a handful of permanent inhabitants, but entertainments continued round the year, as befitted a family seat, with festivals, betrothals, marriages, *shraddhs*, births and deaths at home and abroad.

The girls came and went annually, individually or in groups, daughters, sisters, nieces, nieces of nieces, etc. The house was the hub of the extended family. Although all the boys now lived abroad en famille, they came and went frequently; often the breaks were lengthy stays. At any time, one or more of the boys would be at the residence, if not in person than in the form of wives and kids. However, there were occasions when the resident women were alone and the rancour between them soured the silence of the grand mansion.

Ruth and Reshma and their youthful escorts struggled with the family genealogy and then gave it up. 'Relatives' was an all-inclusive term, to be skipped so as to head for sightseeing and shopping. The heavy silks and embroidered *saris* and *ghaghras* had Ruth in ecstasy.

"How will I carry all this?" she asked her grandmother.

"Don't worry; it will all be shipped to your home."

When the photographs were to be taken, Maya moved pointedly away to her room and closed the door firmly. No one said a word. Ruth stored it all away in her diary, promising herself she would ask Maman, who perhaps knew less. She had never been to India. Pa, it would have to be then. On the last day, there was a lavish feast as the whole family congregated at the Big House. Maya stayed away, as usual. No one commented. Ruth noted.

Why?

That question haunted the entire visit. The girls were well brought up. Courteous and cheerful, they treated Maya with the same grave, yet affectionate courtesy they accorded their grandmother and other elderly relatives, giving away nothing about their mental queries. Who was she? What role did she play in Grandma's household? Yes, they knew it was their grandma's household.

Several times in those seemingly never-ending days, Maya was tempted to broach the subject, to probe. What had they been told, by Shyam, or by Rose? Better to clear the air for once and for always. But her courage deserted her. She pursed her lips as the swirl of engagements swept the youngsters through several establishments, for breakfast, lunch, tea and dinner and in between.

"Phew! This has been exhausting, for my stomach," complained Ruth. "Ammi, can't we stay home and relax, just for once?"

Ammi's face was troubled. "If you had come for a longer period, you could have relaxed. See, if you don't go to your aunt's house today, after visiting everyone else, she'll be upset and others will start wondering why you didn't go to her house."

"She'll lose face," explained Maya patiently.

"I can understand that. But, is India all about heavy food and relatives? Where are the elephants and snakes, the dances and the temples and all that culture?"

There was a short breathless silence. Maya was non-plussed. She had planned meticulously to keep the girls too occupied with people to find time to raise questions. She had included the visit to the motel to give them a feel of modern India, and here they were asking for a taste of the old.

The concerted, expectant gaze of two pairs of youthful eyes was boring through Maya, as if they were waiting for her response. Even Ammi was. Maya felt helpless. What were they expecting of her? An invitation to stay longer? Had Shyam primed them?

"Everyone comes to India to meet their families and relatives, to eat *desi* food and to shop. I..." she corrected herself, "We knew you didn't have time, so we've bought some things for you. If you want you can shop for more in Bombay."

She got up precipitately to fetch the presents she and Ammi had collected for them...

*****

If the kids' trip was hectic, with an underlay of questioning tension, which Maya felt was hers alone; Rose's visit was nothing but a pure torture – for both of them, with Ammi, Sheel, Dadi and Maya's own sister, Pratima all poised like cats on a hot tin roof.

The run-up to the visit had been equally traumatic. The news had come to Gunwant first, not to Ammi. The poor man was totally flustered as he whispered to Ammi. For once, even the old woman was shaken. For years, she had administered a Sword of Damocles over Maya's head, on Shyam's behalf. In fact, it had been her own well-worked tactic, to ward off mutiny.

Now the actual Sword had fallen, in so many words. Shyam had sent word that Rose was coming to meet her and Maya both and that he did not want any trouble. Gunwant was too dazed to be able to recall Shyam's exact words.

Maya wondered why Gunwant was troubled. She turned to look back as she entered the kitchen, and saw both her brother-in-law and mother-in-law quite agitated. In her wildest dreams, she would not have imagined what Ammi had just heard.

Many times, when Maya allowed her thoughts to go wool gathering, she had thought of Shyam coming home for a visit. She could never imagine him coming back for good. Maya thought up innumerable scenarios of Shyam's visit, meeting her, not meeting her, ignoring her, acknowledging her, sending her away and what not.

However, never had she anticipated that he would send his wife alone instead. After a tense dinner, she found Ammi particularly uneasy.

"What is it, Ammi?"

The old woman was hard put to meet her eyes. Her lips moved almost of their own volition, as she looked up into Maya's huge traumatised eyes. Eyes locked, both of them shrank into their chairs.

"Ammi…"

"What can I do?"

"Ammi, stop him."

"How can I stop him? This is his house. And she is his wife. He wants her to get…."

The old woman's face broke up as the words choked in her throat.

"He wants her to get my blessings."

Poor Ammi! She was torn between her love for her long lost son and her duty to the girl she had plucked out of her parental home and brought into her household, thereby condemning her to a life sentence of rejection. She had, all along, owned total responsibility for Maya.

"She is my *bahu*." It was this moral pressure that had compelled Shyam to acknowledge the woman he had rejected, as his wife.

Within the family, Maya was accepted as Shyam's wife, even if they had never lived together or even consummated the marriage. That was something very few of the old people were privy to. Moreover, they did not broadcast it. Among the younger lot, it was accepted that Maya looked after her mother-in-law, while Shyam earned his millions abroad. And if he chose to take another wife to bed abroad, everyone was sensible enough not to discuss it, except in private. In any case, there was always some other scandal to discuss and this one had carried on for ever so long!

Now, the chickens were coming home to roost. Ammi called in her storm troopers, Dadi and Co, to break the chilly silence into which Maya had withdrawn. She hadn't uttered a word since dinnertime and it was getting past noon the next day. There were less than 48 hours for Rose to arrive.

When the Dadis descended on Maya, they were shocked to the core at the raw passions mirrored in her face. The face was, (if that was possible), darker than before. But they hammered away at her.

"Take control of yourself, Maya. Have you gone mad? How can you stop a man from entering his own home, or sending his wife home? And don't you talk of leaving. Why should you leave your home? For what? Whom? That woman will come, for some hours and go away. And for that, you'll leave Ammi alone for the rest of her life? After all that she has done for you? Is that what you'll do?" Dadi tried to reason with her.

Didi took it up. "Why? You've known all along that Shyam had another wife. That he was married soon after he left you. In spite of that, he looked after you all these years. More than looked after you. Look at yourself. You're better off than most, with a house, like a palace, in your own name. What more can you want?" (All those latent jealousies came creeping out in that harangue.)

"All these years, he never came home once to meet his mother, all because of you. Which son wouldn't want to meet his mother? Have you ever asked Ammi how much she misses her son? But no one has ever said anything to you. Now all he wants is that Rose should get Ammi's blessings. Why is that troubling you? Didn't the children come last year? You made so much noise about it then. But see how well it all went off. The children sang such praises of you and your house. Maybe that is why Rose wants to come – she must have seen the photographs…." That was Bhagwanti.

On and on went the drone. But Maya remained in a frozen trauma, her huge eyes rebuking the speaker until they fell silent.

Left with no option, Dadi grabbed Maya's shoulders and shook her in desperation.

"Why don't you understand, *mari*, you have no option but to receive her?" Speechlessly Maya stood up and shut herself in her own room, leaving the others staring blankly after her.

On the surface, things went off without a hitch. By the time Gunwant brought Rose home from the airport, the house was clean and bright. The fragrance of rose *aggarbattis* and room freshener wafted to the gate.

By common consent, no one else was informed of Rose's arrival. There wasn't the gaggle of aunts, cousins and others at the gate. Only Sheel and the older women, none of the younger set, to escort Rose upstairs.

The 'imported' *bahu* was the picture of Parisian elegance. Only the slant of her eyes and the raven black hair gave away her far eastern blood. Otherwise, the black skirt, the silken blouse and hose, the elegantly shod feet shrieked Paris.

Rose was a voluptuous full-blown rose, in all senses, the match for Shyam that Maya could never be. Her face reflected her personal and her husband's success, oiled and creamed, plucked and plumed, glowing with the sexual wellbeing of a woman well loved.

Sheel and the Dadis had met Rose on her home turf, as Shyam's guests. There had been no Maya there then, to compare and contrast. Here there was. Ammi was seeing Rose for the first time and her photographs had not really done justice to her at all.

In real life, Rose oozed a sensuality that the older woman recognised. Ammi was almost appalled at her own mistake in wanting to thrust Maya into the life of a man whose taste glowed before her. Tears came into the old woman's eyes, as she thought of three lives blighted by her mistake. The onlookers put another construction altogether on Ammi's moist eyes.

Rose had been well primed. As she entered the house and saw Ammi on her *divan*, she swept off the black and silver scarf from her shoulders, draped it carefully over her head and wound the ends around her neck. As she approached the old woman, she bent deep and touched her feet in respect. She waited those few seconds with head bent and fingers touching the toes, to feel the old woman's hand touch her head in blessing.

Gunwant clicked away happily. Maya was nowhere in sight. The Dadis exchanged apprehensive looks. No one could quite control Maya, could they?

With a cheerful smile, Ammi shepherded everyone into the drawing room.

"Come, come, let's have tea first."

As they entered, the Dadis sighed with relief. Maya was there, her back to them as she organised the setting of the tea table, pulling in dishes through the hatch to settle them just so, on the large table. There was the usual generous Maya spread, a blend of desi *samosas* and *pakoras*, with pastries and wafer thin cucumber sandwiches.

Maya looked cool and queenly, with her trademark pearls setting off a lime green chiffon *sari*, massive green roses adorning her *pallu* and the top pleat. The large one slashing across her frail chest was The Irony, as she turned to face her real 'Rose' counterpart. Not all the careful makeup could disguise Maya's enormous wounded eyes, bleeding out her trauma – the ignominy of being spurned, of being ground to heel by entertaining Rose in her home, not of her own free will, but at the dictate of the one who had spurned her. It was as if her broken heart filled those wounded eyes.

The two women faced each other for an eternity, it seemed. The full blown rose and the Tragic Queen. As Rose read Maya's eyes, her cheerful demeanour drained out of her face, leaving it almost waxen.

Maya's voice was dull but carefully controlled.

"Would you like to freshen up before sitting down for tea?" she asked in careful English. Graciously, she led Rose to the guestroom. Very much the Lady of the Manor, she left her at the door of the room, leaving Rose to appreciate the pale yellow walls and autumnal gold in the drapes and bedspread.

"Excellent taste," thought Rose, as she eyed the stained glass bedside lamps, "expensive too, from our top class luxury range." The thought came automatically as she methodically washed her hands and touched up lipstick and hair. Maya's eyes had sabotaged her calm and it took several deep breaths to clear the system, before she stepped back into the drawing room.

Conversation stilled at her footfall. Maya was presiding over the table, serving Ammi, the Dadis, Gunwant and his wife. She motioned Rose to the table with her hand, to fill her plate. Her eyes were carefully averted. Rose breathed easy, not for long.

Hardly had she sat down carefully next to Ammi and picked a bite from her sandwich, Maya brought Rose her tea. The two sat facing each other, looking deep into each other's eyes, plumbing the depths of unspoken emotions. As the wordless probing continued, the silence stilled everyone around them.

For the two main protagonists, Maya and Rose, it was heart-wrenching time. They looked deep into each other's eyes, reading the questions, the sorrow, the defeat, the triumph and finally the pleading and the sympathy. But they hardly uttered a word.

What was there to say? Between an abandoned wife, who was, nevertheless, accepted as Mrs. Shyam and the Lover Woman who had won her Man with her love... sex... money... who lived and worked shoulder to shoulder with him and had borne him children.

As they sat across the table, sharing a pot of tea, the contrast between them was sharp. Maya, for all her regal chiffon and pearls, could do little to disguise the toll of the decades on her face. Unloved, untouched by any man, her figure was still virginal, her face pinched with the present tension. Huge sad eyes set in enormous dark circles dominated the gaunt face. Her fingers flashed diamond rings, but they were fleshless and bony.

Across the table from her was Juno personified, a full blown rose. Her make up was immaculate, discreet diamonds shone at her ears, throat and fingers; an exquisite silk suit matched Maya's ensemble. The voluptuous figure and the face were that of a woman who had had all the sex that she had wanted or needed. A contented face with that special glow which stood out amongst all the aunts and cousins who spent a lifetime waiting for their men; the glow which could not be replicated from any of the innumerable creams and lotions that loaded the dressing tables of the inhabitants of the city of crones.

The Dadis thanked their stars that no one else was present. Even Sheel and Gunwant were temporarily out of the room. In fact, it was their noisy re-entry that broke the spell. Rose shook her head, as if to reorient herself. She put down her cup. Leaning forward, she placed both her hands on Maya's bony hands. Her lips mouthed something soundlessly – no one heard the words, the intent was clear.

Finally, Maya's tortured eyes closed. A trickle seeped through. But before she could humiliate herself full and break down, Rose swung round. Taking Gunwant by the arm, she led him out. Dadi went to join them and in very short order, Rose left with Gunwant, promising to be in time for dinner. Ammi insisted.

Unable to cope with the raw emotions in Maya's face, Rose took refuge in a hotel room for her short stay. She came and went from the house, to renew friendships with family members who had been her guests and to shop.

Maya was a careful and gracious hostess. However, they were unable to go forward together. After having broken the ice, they stood frozen on the two sides of the broken ice, immobilised by 'what may have been' their own insecurities.

Why are women always insecure?

Rose had everything going for her. She had saved Shyam's life during the War. Her inheritance had provided Shyam with his financial backbone, for which he would always be indebted to her. Quite apart from the business, there was a strong bond between them. That had been evident to the whole family that had gone to visit them. It was another matter altogether that no one had ever spoken about it in Maya's presence, but she always knew. But why was Rose dwarfed by Maya's agony?

Why is it that women always feel insecure, even in their triumph? What is it that their men hold over them? A woman, who has proved her love for her man over and over again, still is subjected to and allows herself to be subjected to tests. 'If you really love me, do this... that... wear this, meet that....' Who has the courage to stand up and say, 'Enough. No more tests. Now I will test you.' The men always back down before a test. Their plethora of excuses are limitless.

Shyam had sent Rose purposely to get his mother's blessings, knowing fully well that Ammi was living with Maya. Had Rose ever put him through any such tests of love and loyalty before she saved him from the Japanese, and ever after? Did she say, "If you love me, stop sending money for Maya?" What would Shyam have done then?

Man can take an almost careless sadistic pleasure in exposing his woman to the most excruciating experiences, merely perhaps to satisfy his ego. The woman will move heaven and earth to protect him from the emotional trauma. He always wants his woman to understand him and his needs, cater to his weaknesses, but does he extend similar support to his wife as well?

*****

3

BABA AND BHARTI

Ammi was always anxious about her sons. There was never that level of concern about Baba. Had anyone else ever wondered why?

As far back as anyone could remember, they rarely ever spoke to each other. It was difficult to imagine Baba and Ammi as a married couple, as parents. Baba was a rarity in this commercial minded community of traders – a person who thought, ruminated, wrote and explored ideas.

When Baba was about seven or eight, during a rare outing to some *dargah*, he had met a *dervish*, handing out potions of herbs and powders to the sick who came to him with their ailments. The little boy got fascinated, as one by one, people narrated their woes. The old man listened intently, asked some questions and put together remedies. When the rush slackened, the little boy approached the old man with his own questions. Baba was tracked down hours later, still listening intently on the old man expounding his philosophy. He was quickly dragged away.

And that would have been that, but for the chance that brought the *Fakir* wandering into the *mohalla*, singing his mesmeric chant to the beat of his '*chimta*', long iron tongs clanging against his iron *kadas*. Baba was captivated. Thenceforth, he followed the *Fakir* around, became his keen disciple and bore thrashings at home stoically.

Eventually he was packed off abroad on a premature first job in foreign lands. There too, Baba continued his readings – itself a rarity. He explored the foreign lands he visited for the types of herbs and powders he had seen with the Fakir, or their equivalents and learnt more. Coming back home, his wandering threw him in the company of a beautiful girl, Rajjo, who was everything a bride should be, shy, homely, beautiful, and fair – but a Muslim. There was consternation on all fronts.

It was to distract that flow of Baba's life that he was married off in a very short order to a young heiress. It was a wise move, for it was evident to all that Baba was no businessman and would earn no fortune abroad. The heiress was beautiful and intelligent. She understood the situation she was pitched into. She did not rebel overtly. However, she was also very proud. Such a pride drove in the wedges and kept them there.

"Come and listen to these poems which I am reading," Baba invited his heiress.

"Who gave you that book?" she asked suspiciously.

"A friend."

"The *mussalmaani*?"

"No. Her name is Rajjo."

"Did I ask? What is she to me?" and she went off.

Tragedy stalked the ill-starred couple. The heiress had been told about Rajjo – but not counselled on how to win over her intellectual husband with some mellowness, rather than her haughty pride.

Baba slunk away to his old job in Rangoon, to surface a good three years later, to the rousing welcome accorded to the prodigal sons. Baba and his heiress barely rubbed along, dutifully producing two sons and a daughter before pointedly calling it a day. He spent longer and longer years abroad. Baba was not there when his children grew up, not even when his first-born Shyam married. He never knew how his wife graduated from being 'the heiress' to Ammi for the whole family.

The relation between Baba and Ammi was enigmatic.

"What is so great in these books, which do not earn any money? Go and make a deal somewhere, instead of this," Ammi would demand.

She no doubt resented being made to feel inferior to Baba's scholarship, now widely acknowledged. She trivialised it while reveling in her position in the extended family. Whenever there was a shortfall because of Baba's bad deals, she would fall back on her personal resources to keep up appearances even within the family. Baba more or less left her to her own devices, rarely if ever interfering with her decisions.

Was that perhaps why Ammi was so complacent about Shyam's rejection of Maya? And therefore, vehement in defending Maya's status within the family, as Shyam's legal wedded wife? Did she believe that eventually her son would take after his father?

The only time Baba raised his voice was after his return from Rangoon for the first time after Shyam had married and abandoned Maya. No one knew why Ammi had selected Maya in the first place. Granted that Shyam was not a good looker, but he was intelligent, he worked hard and unlike his father, had a knack for making money. Moreover, he belonged to a highly respected family.

In the limited privacy of their own room in the old Hyderabad house, Baba had lambasted Ammi. "Why, just tell me, why did you have to do this? Was one tragedy not enough for you that you wanted to repeat it? Now your son has gone off, leaving you with his bride. He drinks a lot and gets into endless trouble. Until he sobers down, it will be your duty, since you selected the bride, to look after her and ensure that no one slights her.

If I hear from anyone anywhere that she had been slighted, I shall personally hold you responsible."

The threat worked well. In this little community of endless tangled networks spread across the seven seas, it was entirely possible to get news of anyone from just about anyone anywhere. Obviously, Baba had news of Shyam, but after that nocturnal explosion, no one dared to ask him. He left soon thereafter, unable to stand the pettishness at home and the stifling political acrimony over the splitting of the country.

Ammi set about tracking down Shyam through the vast family network, but the War intervened and there was no news to be had of anyone for a long time.

Years later, Baba came home for good after a long illness, debilitated and prematurely grey. That was the first time he saw Bharti, lying comatose on her bed, tiny, frail, head shaven and spittle dribbling out of her mouth.

"Why didn't you write to me?" he demanded.

"What would you have done?" countered Ammi.

Baba fell silent. "What happened?"

"None of you men were there when we had to leave for India. There were just Vadi Amma and I to bring the family over as best we could," she told him.

Partition was a nightmare smothered in silence. Everyone talked about it but left out the details.

"*Hai kya zamana tha! Kitna dar tha!* At each station, they took different things. First, it was gold, chains, bangles, earrings, rings, guineas, silver cash… sewing machines at one station, *razais* at another, clocks at another, watches, even *lotas*… what was left…" Then the memories would trail off into silence and a change of subject.

At each station, they were robbed, so that they arrived with little more than the multiple clothes on their backs. The family had a lot to thank the Big House for. One of the oldest brothers had had the foresight of starting a Khadi business near Bombay, right from the time that Gandhiji had made the new fabric a fashion as well as a nationalist statement.

The Big House sheltered all those who made it across the Partition, and helped them to shift into their own quarters, funded by the money that was sent in from all the corners of the globe by the men abroad. In no time at all, the Big House was the hub of a settlement that boasted of the best of treasures from across the seven seas, to replace the treasures left behind.

Beyond that, there was a conspiracy of silence over the Partition. Women talked sometimes about their homes left behind and about what they were robbed off enroute, but not what they brought with them, in their traumatised minds. No one talked about the mobs they saw, the murders, and the mayhem. No one even probed much.

The evidence was there before their eyes, looming large in the midst of the house – a wasting beauty, daughter of the house lying comatose, each day gnawing away at her once acclaimed beauty, her vitriolic tongue stilled forever. As hope for Bharti's recovery dwindled, her vacant eyes moved frantically, her hands switching uncertainly at her sides. Her locks were shorn off to ward off the successive attacks of lice. Bharti had passed into the realm of the forgotten and neither mother, nor sisters nor bhabhis would say what had brought the lovely one to this pass. "*Hai lagi kisi ki*," they would say with eyes averted.

*****

The train journey for the Partition was a living horror, as all the ladies huddled together, clutching pitiful bundles and the children in tight well-knit groups, all bundled into several sets of clothes one over the other. Their male escort was in a pitiable condition, as all the men were abroad, there were just a few little boys and a couple of men servants who cowered, if anything, more than the young girls.

It was while Vadi Amma was railing at them to show more manhood that Bharti slipped away. Bharti was the baby vixen of the family; she was petite and fair, grey eyed and prettier than Sita, sharper of tongue, the bane of the lives of all her bhabhis with her demanding ways, her sharp repartee and her over-confidence.

Bharti strode into the next carriage to a chorus of calls, "Bharti, Bharti, don't go there." She ignored them. Seconds later, before Vadi Amma completed her sentence to her old cook and turned around to call Bharti, her shrieks were ringing through the carriage.

Grabbing her cook by the arm, Vadi Amma raced across. Too late. There were bits and pieces of Bharti's clothes in the passageway. She was not quite visible in the flail of arms and legs and bottoms. Only her shrieks could be heard, which died down to gasps and then to animal moans. A goon with a naked sword and a huge smirk stood guard for an eternity.

When Vadi Amma returned carrying a pitiful mass of flesh, blood and wild eyes emitting animal cries, her hair was white and her faced aged beyond recognition. Her eyes rolled around in terror as she held the child close. They cleaned Bharti as best they could and wrapped her in a clean *sari*, folding her flailing arms tightly, as they would have swaddled a new borne babe.

When the first reaction set in and both Vadi Amma and Bharti broke out in shivers, they were covered in all the available *shawls*. Everyone took turns at rubbing Vadi Amma's hands and feet, which were as cold as ice.

Delhi was a nightmare, flooded with refugees. With Vadi Amma being out of commission, along with a bleeding patient, it was

Baba's Heiress, who became universally Ammi, to take charge of the whole group, commandeering space in trains and trucks and buses, anything to reach them to their destination, the Family Mansion, later known as the Big House.

It was fortunate that Ammi had stowed away her own and her *bahu's* ample collection of gold guineas and jewels in a money belt around her person and had also parcelled some around to Vadi Amma and the other women. This was a boon in transit. By the time the journey ended, new equations had been formed in the family. Vadi Amma and Bharti, it was obvious, would need prolonged medical care. Among the older women, none wanted the responsibility of taking decisions, only of carping. Ammi ignored them. Among the *bahus* and *betis*, she found doers and followers and used them to keep the herd together, ruthlessly at times. Her *bahu*, Maya, was extremely biddable and a stolid rock on whom the younger ones leaned. Ammi used her to deal with the officialdom at the railway and the bus stations, safe in the knowledge that no Bharti-like fate would attach itself to her.

Baba was shattered over Bharti's fate. He took it upon himself to sit with her for hours, talking to her, reading from his treatises, even singing. She seemed to be happy after it.

For their parts, Baba and Ammi were happier keeping each other at an arm's length. Perhaps, with the passage of time, both regretted their getting-off-on-a-wrong foot, but knew not how to affect a rollback.

Baba was burdened by the guilt of not being there for Bharti, Ammi by her guilt for her role in Maya's fate. They avoided each other.

Baba was immersed in his books, potions, and Bharti. Ammi was busy with her hopes for Maya and her own role as a family matriarch.

Vadi Amma could never recover from her vision of how Bharti was gang raped before her very eyes. Prolonged treatments, medicines, *buas* and even electric shocks became part of her life and those of the *bahus* and *betis* who attended to her. When she was fine, Vadi Amma kept the Big House on its toes, smiling cheerfully as she did her '*seva*' of her '*thakurs*', bathing the small silver idols with milk and water, anointing them with sandal paste, adorning them with tiny sequined garments and garlands of flowers before rounding off with a soft toned *aarti*, all interspersed with loud commands to all and sundry, the cook, the maids, the *bahus*, the *betis* and the grand *betis*.

However, when the old memories came to haunt Vadi Amma, her long silver locks flailed around as she swung her head from side to side, rolling her eyes and pleading piteously, "*Bas, bas, bas, bas, bas...*" It was days before normalcy would be restored in the household.

By common consensus, it was decided, "Let Bharti go in the new house where Vadi Amma will not see her every day and be troubled by her memories."

Maya's famous tact saw Baba and Bharti settled in one wing of the ground floor of the new villa, designed specially for them. This arrangement also provided privacy to Gunwant and Sheel who lived in the opposite wing of the ground floor, while Ammi and Maya took over the upper floor.

Bharti's room opened into Baba's so he could supervise her daily routine, the exercises, the massage and the diet by the maids while sitting at his desk. Outside was a long verandah populated by his ancient wooden chair with a cane netting. As he sat on it, he could look out to his little enclosed garden where he grew herbs for his very-much-in-demand potions. It was another matter altogether that the demand was more from the outsiders than his family.

Maya had arranged a special plot for him, away from her own little Japanese garden, knowing that Baba loved to potter around by himself. Occasionally someone would pop in to seek his advice on some herbal remedy or the homeopathy pills, which he also dispensed. Baba always responded self-depreciatingly, diffident at any self-propagation and wary perhaps of ridicule from closer home. This was the case from not only Ammi, who only very late learnt to forgive her fate. Many others loved nothing better to strike out at the harmless old man; sometimes it was to assuage their own feelings of superiority over a man who was so different from the average, and sometimes merely for the pleasure of rubbing up Ammi and her sense of superiority.

Less than a week after Bharti's funeral, Baba collapsed in his garden while pottering around his beloved plants. His face was turned to the sun, calm and serene in the knowledge that his tasks on earth were complete.

*****

4

MAYA'S SISTER

A graceful figure sitting near the front of the funeral gathering evinced more than the nominal grief which was on display on most faces. Padma was tall and slim; her delicate features bore a startling resemblance to the woman who was being mourned, only the combination was so much more pleasing than the gaunt look that was typical of Maya. Padma was Maya's younger sister, genuinely upset at the loss of her sister. Her smart young daughter, Lavina sat quietly next to her.

Padma too had a tough time in her marriage. Her situation was the opposite of that of Maya, but perhaps she was luckier than the most, especially Maya, as the situation did not carry on for too long. Within a few years, she and her husband had found a meeting ground. They then continued from there on to be one of the most notable 'happily ever after marriages' that the family could boast of.

It had been an arranged marriage too, just like Maya's. And again it was the old people on both sides who did the 'seeing', neither the groom, nor the bride. Padma's daughter often rebelled at that very thought.

*****

"I want someone I can relate to, whom I cannot merely grow old with, but also share a romantic honeymoon, repeatedly.

Social values are important, so is romance... a dreamy wedding night...."

Lavina clutched her arms in shivery excitement as her dark doe eyes assessed the photographs on the table before her. The eyes narrowed over the printouts under each picture, the biodata details which revealed as much or as little as the photographs.

Her mother's shiver was involuntary. "A wedding night is quite often a trauma. Don't go by your M&B." (Mills & Boons novels)

The tone was sharp enough to make Lavina look up, gazing speculatively at her. "Why do you say that?"

Her mother hesitated. "Isn't it obvious? One gets exhausted after all those festivities and excitement and emotional upheaval. Where is the question of being at one's best relaxed self? How is it possible to relax, with a total stranger, following a strange ritual?"

"A strange ritual? What are you talking about, ma?

"Isn't the whole *suhaag raat* business a ritual also? To be enacted for the 'feel-good' factor of family, friends, society and all?"

Lavina protested. "How can you say that, ma..." but after a pause, she sat next to her mother and asked curiously, "Tell me, Ma, what was it like?"

"What?" asked her mother.

"The *suhaag raat* of yours."

A shadow flitted across the older woman's face, breaking up with a remembered pain that Lavina had never seen on her face before. She knew that her parents were mismatched. That they had survived past a silver anniversary was entirely thanks to their old world values and stiff upper lip upbringing, revolving around upholding family secrets and to that old bugbear, "*Ghar ki baat ghar ki char deewaron mein hi rahani chahiye.*"

It took some coaxing, but eventually the older woman relaxed. Was it an urge to unburden? Or a mother's desire to warn her daughter of the dangers ahead? Padma started in a small voice.

"We had never met. It was not done in those days, in our families. My family had seen him and your Papa's family came to see me."

"Did you carry the tea tray?" prompted Lavina gaily.

"Don't be silly. That is not for people like us. But yes, they did find an excuse to make me walk about, after checking my high heels, just to make sure that I was not a *langdi* (lame). And of course, they made me speak Hindi and English to check the language and the diction as well. They checked out my eyes, my jewellery and the brand name on my handbag. If only there were X-ray eyes, maybe they'd have checked out my insides too."

"Then the wedding happened. I know all that, I've seen the album. What after…" Lavina was getting impatient.

Her mother was reflective, apprehensive over how much to lay bare. It was difficult despite her decision that her daughter should know.

"I got the shock of my life when your father lifted my *ghunghat*." Padma shuddered involuntarily. "Everyone had kept on saying that he was *Rajkumar*. I was expecting a *Rajkumar*, tall, fair and handsome."

"Oh my God…" Lavina's hands flew to her mouth, "That is why… you are tall, slim, fair and delicate; and Pa, tall yes, but dark, those scary bloodshot eyes, pock marks on his cheeks and forehead and that wonderful swashbuckling *mooch* of his!!"

Lavina guiltily remembered the nocturnal sessions with her siblings and cousins, revolving around 'the beauty and the beast' speculations.

"Can you imagine what I went through in those seconds? There was I, bone tired, hungry and obviously scared with anticipation of what next? No one tells it all before hand. And then I see this, this apparition...." Padma put out her hands in a pleading gesture.

"What did you do?"

"It was quite unforgivable. I fainted."

"Fainted?"

"Uh huh, just passed out on the bed. When I came to my senses, the *ghunghat* was back on my face and your father was nowhere to be seen."

"Then?" breathed Lavina.

"I was scared out of my wits, obviously."

"But where was he?"

"Lord knew. I didn't see him all day. In the evening..."

Padma went back in time.

The evening after the wedding was a big dinner, hosted at the club. When her mother-in-law told her to go and get dressed for it, she went with some trepidation, expecting Raj to be in the room. She sighed with relief, when she found no one there. But soon enough, the maids and hair-dresser were swarming over her.

Raj walked stiffly into the room. Their eyes met in the mirror. Turning on his heel, he picked out a suit from his cupboard and walked out.

They arrived at the club together, without exchanging a word, only wary glances. On the way home, when Raj put out his hand to cover hers, Padma shivered. He withdrew his hand.

Two more days of the cat and mouse game left her pale enough not to go unnoticed. The honeymoon in Kashmir metamorphosed into a short business trip for Raj. When she heard about it, Padma heaved a sigh of relief and encountered the yearning in Raj's eyes and a steely look in her mother-in-law's. She looked desperately for escape, but there was none.

As soon as Raj left, and she had offered a stiff 'bon voyage' in the privacy of their room, Padma was summoned by the old woman.

They sat on the huge old-fashioned bed, facing each other. The look in the older woman's eyes was no longer steely but sorrowful.

"Has he hurt you?" she probed and Padma was caught off guard.

"No, no; who said so?" she countered warily.

"I'm just asking. Why are you against Raj?"

"Who said so? I'm not against him."

"But you act as if you're frightened of him. You shiver and pale when he sits next to you. I know he has not touched you yet..."

Padma looked up startled. "How?"

"Everyone knows. It is so obvious. Why do you think Raj has been sent on a business trip instead of a honeymoon? The servants did not have to change your bed sheets once."

Padma was mortified. She did not know the exact significance of the failure to change the bed sheets. But she was surprised by the fact that the servants were privy to her bedroom affairs.

Her mother-in-law's tone became gentler. "Tell me, *bahu*, what is the problem? Did he say something to upset you? What is disturbing you?"

The soft touch brought Padma to tears as her floodgates burst.

"No one warned me. How was I to know?"

"Know what?" the older woman was genuinely clueless.

Padma did not know how to say it. She gasped and hummed-hawed, clenching and unclenching her hands helplessly.

"Why don't you start from the beginning?" prompted the old lady.

Padma's look was piteous. She was sorry for herself, of being caught in this mess, furious with herself for being unable to handle the situation and at her mother for not even warning her of what to expect and embarrassed over how to reveal all of this to her mother-in-law.

Why hadn't Raj told his mother, for Heaven's sake?

"Was it before or after the marriage?" asked the older woman.

Padma looked at her helplessly. "Before... no after... maybe before..."

"Make up your mind please. Before or after?"

"Both," said Padma with a small finality.

"Both?" now the old woman was confused.

When did they meet before the wedding, she thought.

Padma took a deep breath.

The old lady shrewdly placed the issue in her lap.

"Whatever is the problem between you two, I am sure that you can sit together and resolve it. *Bahu*, you have just got married. You two have a long way to go... with the blessings of all your elders."

She looked deep into the younger woman's eyes and resumed, "I am sure you would not want your parents to worry about you all the time."

Padma got the point immediately. If the news of an obviously unresolved issue went back to her maternal home, it could only mean trouble, worry and dishonour for her parents. In their conservative society, there was no shame greater than that of a married daughter being sent back to her parental home by her in-laws and her husband. One Maya in the family was bad enough for her parents.

Padma bowed her head to touch her mother-in-law's feet and withdrew to her own room.

So, Raj had said nothing. Why? To protect his own ego? Why should he acknowledge to anyone that his looks had put off his bride? Padma tossed her head.

But soon enough sobering thoughts prevailed.

Was it looks alone that counted? He could have shamed her with a cooked up tale of her inadequacy or he could have forced himself on her or sent her back home. He had done none of that. He'd just left quietly, without saying a word.

Padma sat playing out the entire chain of events since the wedding in her mind's eye. Her father and Phuphi's stern warnings resounded in her brain, "*Yaad rahe. Ghar ki baat hamesha ghar ki char deewaron me hi rahe.*"

"*Maike ki laaj ab tere haathon mein hain. Naak katwaigi to sarr kaat doonga.*"

Each was more ominous than the next. She felt drained. What to do?

Her mother-in-law's words came back to her "Whatever is the problem between you two, I am sure that you can sit together and resolve it."

"I'll have to wait for Raj to come home." She started strengthening herself to meet her husband and talk to him.

Raj came home after a long while. Somehow he did not look so intimidating now. Perhaps because she was prepared for him and his looks. Perhaps it was the absence of the flower bedecked bed, her heavy clothes, the *achkan* and that atmosphere. He seemed somewhat approachable.

Padma gave him a tremulous smile of welcome. His mother put a hand on Raj's arm to take him aside for a whispered exchange.

After dinner, they faced each other. He cocked a bushy eyebrow. "Did you miss me?"

Padma was confused. More than a little pink in cheek, she nodded, "Maybe... a little."

"I've brought something for you," curiosity killed the kitten as he drew out a peace offering.

*****

"Then?"

"Then what?"

"Is that how you fell in love with Pa?"

"*Arre bachchi*! Everyone does not go around falling in love. What is this LOVE? A physical thing? Scientists insist it is a chemical reaction. Life is different."

"But don't you love Pa?" Lavina was almost petulant and insistent.

"Yes. I love your Pa – for his honesty, his gentleness, his ability to make me feel good, even better. Getting to know each other and adjust to each other is a long drawn out process after marriage. You know why it is only after marriage? Because before marriage, even after falling love, one has the option to opt out. That option closes the day you marry. So willy-nilly you learn to adjust."

"But there is always an option of divorce..."

"Chhe," the older woman was peremptory in waving that option away, "Not in our families. But *beta* do you know when I actually fell in love with your father?"

"When?" Lavina breathed out.

"The day you were to be born..."

Once again the scenes played themselves out before her eyes as she recalled her past for her daughter.

"I fell in love with Raj when he was overruling all those old hags at my birthing bed."

Two of his old aunts were arguing. "It is not a favourable time for childbirth. Don't let the doctor operate to bring out the baby today."

The doctor was stern. "If we delay it, both the mother and the baby will be in danger."

My mother asked, "What can be worse than losing a child, mine or my daughter's?"

But the old women persisted, "If the child dies, it will be a relief from a life long misery, rather than a long life burdened with *rahu kaal* and *shani*."

That is when Raj walked in. He brushed everyone aside and told the doctor firmly, "Operate right now. I want both the mother and the child."

"Is that why I have all that *mangal, rahu, shani-phani* in my *kundli*?"

"Yes."

"But Pa still loves me."

"Yes he does. So do I. We both do. That also means that we are going to be extra careful in finding a match for you. So that the evil witches' prophecy does not come true. One of the reasons why we shifted our base to Hong Kong."

"But even abroad people are concerned about matching *kundlis*, are they not?"

"That may never change. But you did have a childhood without old fogies pointing to your *kundli* all the time, didn't you?"

*****

5

NEELIMA

A beautiful figure stood out at Maya's funeral. She stood tall, despite a bare 5'3"; she was well rounded, with a long bare neck, deep neckline, well maintained hands and feet, dripping diamonds, a round cheerful face dominated by those blue eyes which gave her the name, Neelima.

She sat with her three daughters, the family resemblance was evident enough. Neelima looked around her with the hint of a slight smile on her face, subdued by the occasion. The smile was acknowledged by the slight nods by virtually everyone. Only on Dadi's face was there chagrin.

As it always was when any of her strong-minded bhabhis or nieces came to visit...

Distance, they say, makes the heart grow fonder. Dadi loved all her relatives when they were abroad. She often expounded on her fond memories of each and every one of them in turn, recalling incidents in the past, showing off their positive traits. But when they descended on the family mansion, it was another story altogether. Petty differences were blown up totally out of proportion. It usually started with the opening of the bags.

What was there in those bags? Clothes, usually by the dozen, of every shape and size – *saris*, dresses, tops, skirts, t-shirts, scarves, shirts, etc. Then came purses, cosmetics, trinkets, toys and chocolates for the little ones, medications like balm and digestives, cameras, radios and then came the real stuff, electronic items, crystal ware, perfumes and a host of other gifts.

Who would decide who should get what? And how much? That was always a dilemma and the arbitrator earned minus points all round. Tough luck, but Dadi loved the power, the leverage attached to being the official opener of the bags and the distributor of the goodies. If the bhabhis resented the leverage she earned out of the trunks brought home by their husbands, tough luck. Dadi's skin was thick enough to take that. And at times, grand tussles with the bhabhis, who would wish to reserve some of the better stuff for their own relatives, only to have Dadi pounce mercilessly; never mind if she later decided that diplomacy called for the bhabhi's sister, bhabhi, or niece to be given something really nice and expensive.

"Okay, keep these things for them. Otherwise, your people will say that your husband is bankrupt and cannot afford nice, expensive things. We'll manage with some of the junk you've brought. One would have thought that after all these years, you would have learnt how to do shopping properly," Dadi would often jibe.

Neelima had come after too long to bother about such pinpricks. She, in fact, was relieved to hand over the keys to all her suitcases, save the one with her personal clothes, and let Dadi decide the gift giving for her. She was neither staying at home, nor did she want to stay in her *sasural*. She had opted to put up in a hotel conveniently close to both the houses, making her neutral position crystal clear to all concerned.

Sitting in the threadbare room dominated by the *Guru Granth Sahib*, Neelima was breathing in her past and reliving old memories silently. She remembered little of the flight from Pakistan as a child. Clinging to her mother's *pallu* while the latter hung on to a baby, Neelima understood little of what had happened to Bharti and Vadi Amma. The aunts in Haridwar were only names to her.

What she remembered clearly of her childhood was her mother, Bhagwanti, abandoned by her father. Until her teens, Neelima could not remember seeing her father. "What did he look like?" There were no photographs of him, but she knew her Dada had come home once, because she had a younger brother. She always hated it when Vadi Amma and Dadi railed at her mother for 'driving away' her Dada.

Neelima had grown up in a household of women, with males as occasional visitors, to be pampered, served, and sent off. Males, uncles, cousins, whatever, did not fit into her life. They were never there when there was a crisis or when they were needed. So everyone learned to do without the male presence. Dadi and Maya aunty did all the official work, paying taxes, going to the municipality, the electricity office, getting school admissions, the banks, purchases, whatever. The boys went off abroad long before they even hit sixteen, so where was the question of having a broad brotherly shoulder to lean on, to question why the occasional visiting male did not include her father, why this or why that?

Neelima was in her last year of school. She was the prefect of her class and was tremendously proud of it, when the news came that Dada was coming for a visit. After all these years, he wanted to come home and see Vadi Amma once. The whole family was excited, as the Prodigal Son was returning. Coming away from his fancy French wife and family in Paris, whom no one had seen or met.

"Could it be so?" wondered Neelima now. "Surely one of the uncles must have dropped in and met them, but did not tell at home for the fear of sparking off a storm unnecessarily," she concluded.

Her Dada turned out to be tall and handsome, even if somewhat rotund, greying elegantly at the temples. Around his eyes was a splay of fine laughter lines, only Neelima did not know then that they were laughter lines. She longed to smoothen those lines away, to see how a youthful Dada may have looked.

And Dada fell in love with his lovely daughter. All the while he was talking to Vadi Amma or Dadi or any of the others who trooped in to meet the Long Lost Son, Dada's eyes followed Neelima, as if drinking in her beauty and reminding himself that she was his own daughter. It was the first time Neelima actually saw a male lay down the law, "As soon as she finishes school, send Neelima to me in Paris."

A storm broke, loud, boisterous and raucous. All of Bhagwanti's grievances that she had been expressly told to keep in check for the duration of this precious visit came tumbling out and at the end of her recital came the final blow, "Now, look, he wants to take my daughter away. First, he left me in the lurch for some whore, now he wants to take my daughter away to her, to teach her what? What will Neelima do in Paris? Her home is here, what is there for her to do?"

The glow in Neelima's heart began to dim. But Dada was adamant. He turned away from his dumpy wife to face his mother and sister.

"Neelima is my daughter. I want her to see the world before she settles down. She deserves a holiday abroad. And why should she not come to her father's house? None of you ever came to see me. I have never complained. But I want my daughter to see the world with my eyes and she shall come. Better make all the arrangements and keep her passport ready. I will send her the visa and the ticket." There was a finality in the tone that no one, neither Vadi Amma nor Dadi, not even Ammi sought out to challenge.

Neelima was in seventh heaven. The very first night in Paris, she made an important discovery. She saw her father laugh. It was a gay, carefree laughter, which brought smiles to the faces that were merely looking on. How can Dada laugh so freely?

Neelima had spent the day with the women of her new family, stepmother Yvette and her step-sister Yvonne. "Today we'll go to the parlour," announced Yvette.

"For what?" Neelima asked anxiously.

"Plenty of things. First of all, that oil has to be washed out of your hair and it will be styled elegantly. Then your arms and legs will be waxed and pampered, along with your face. And then we'll shop."

It did sound a bit daunting to Neelima, but it was one more new experience and when she finally emerged, she felt totally invigorated. The shopping that followed created a brand new Neelima, wearing a short dress with heeled sandals and a smart bag.

Finally, Dada joined them and whistled in appreciation at the apparition that she was his daughter. Now they were sitting at a small bistro, serenaded by a guitarist. She heard the rapid fire French of her stepmother, apparently describing the day. Then she said something and both Dada and Yvette broke up in a gay laughter.

This was a totally new feeling for Neelima. She could not remember seeing Dada laugh so freely at home. Or for that matter, a man and a woman laughing like this?

At home, the women giggled copiously. Men shared their own jokes, at times. She had seen sisters laughing with their brothers at times. Occasionally, at the weddings and other occasions, bawdy songs were sung by the *hijras* and off-colour jokes were told to the bride on the day after, although the same may have been out of bounds the very previous night! But that was different some how.

This joyous sound was so new, so thrilling that all of a sudden; she understood why Dada did not come home. He was free here, to live and to laugh with his woman in a way, which Neelima understood, her mother would never even dream of participating in or enjoying, or allowing him to enjoy.

"I'll never leave my man alone to enjoy his life with another woman. I'll laugh with him," Neelima swore to herself.

Paris was a revelation and a celebration of life. Six months rapidly went by visiting museums, gardens, shops, and exploring French culture. Painting and music transformed Neelima into a confident young woman who was to face a thousand battles, who took the Big House by storm when she went back after succumbing to the 'come home, come home' pressure.

"You betrayed me," her mother raved and ranted all evening. "You went there and did not want to come back to me."

Poor Neelima, unable to cope with her own feelings and her mother's, replied, "I did not betray you, ma. You are my mother and Dada is my father, isn't he. Should I not know him, love him and obey him too?"

However, at the back of her mind, Neelima felt guilty. She knew that mentally she betrayed her mother when she saw her with new eyes.

"Why do you always wear your hair in a thin oily *chuttiya*? Why not a bun or trimmed hair since it is so thin? Doesn't Chachi have short hair? Why do you never laugh, never smile, never... don't you want to wear coloured *saris* ever? So what if relatives die? They are everyone's relatives, not only yours. Other aunties also wear coloured *saris* at times; why do you always wear this boring white?"

For her mother, white was convenient. Everyone knew she had been deserted and that her husband did not come home because he had a foreign wife.

"Why should I bother? White is so convenient, no bothering about selection, what to wear when and in any case, who is there to please or impress? By the time the mourning for one dead relative is over, some other, obscure or otherwise, will go and I have a convenient excuse to save myself the trouble of selecting colours and matching *saris* to the occasion."

Everyone compared her situation with Maya, unfavorably.

"Look at the difference between Maya and Bhagwanti. Maya too is a deserted woman. Bhagwanti has the advantage of having two children, Maya is still a virgin. Yet Maya is always elegantly turned out, tastefully adapting the latest fashions to her spare person; Bhagwanti is always boring and drab in white, never elegantly so."

The next battle started when Neelima expressed her desire to go to college.

"Girls, don't go to college," replied her mother.

"Hundreds of them do. Indira Gandhi was sent to college and that too in England and see where she is today."

"You are not Indira Gandhi. This is not Motilal Nehru's house. If you go to college, how will we find a boy for you? Our boys don't study."

"Yes, they do. Even a Matric pass will do. Dada has told me to go to college and to learn music... to sing *bhajans* properly (that was her own on-the-spur-of-the-moment invention). See, he has already deposited money for my fees." She waved a passbook.

That did the trick – but would these battle-axes ever end? Before she cleared her inter, they found a match no one could say no to, not even Neelima's father.

In those days, eligible boys used to be "For Sale to the Highest Bidder". These guys came from all the corners of the world, Hong Kong, Gibraltar, Eden, Malta, Nigeria, Morocco, Panama, Manila, New York, Saigon, Singapore or whatever.

Weeks before they arrived, concerned relatives and professional matchmakers, would be making offers with 'so and so is offering a couple of diamond bangles'. That was the standard, along with the trousseau and the gold for the girl, suitcases of clothes for the groom and his family, silver vessels, negotiated number of gold guineas and cash or extra ornaments in lieu of bedding etc; plus of course, the actual expenses on festivities which were lavish and as long drawn out or as short as one wanted them to be. If the business was down, there were only two diamond bangles, otherwise much more, plus a complete set with earrings, necklace and one or two rings, in addition to sets of gold, pearls and other precious stones. If the girl was not too fair or beautiful, the dowry obviously increased.

Then a short list was drawn up. When the boy arrived, he went to see the shortlisted candidates. It was for him to say yes or no to the looks offered. What else to gauge in the barely audible, "Hello, I am studying… movies... my favourite is Shammi Kapoor or Sunil Dutt or whatever." A quarter of a century ago, it was like that. It remains that way in the present also, only Shah Rukh and Abhishek have replaced Shammi and Sunil.

Hari was the eldest son of a director of one of the oldest Sindhi trading firm, with branches all over the world. He had grown up aboard, spoke French like a native and was well-educated.

The song in Neelima's heart choked when she remembered her vow. She scanned the faces. Whom could she co-opt as her ally? Ma? No; Vadi Amma in one of her lucid moments – no. The Chachis – doubtful. She zeroed in on Dadi – the biggest battle-axe of them all. Best to have Dadi on her side. Neelima waited for her moment.

"Dadi…"

"*Haan... chao...*"

"Dadi, there is one thing. I can only say it to you. I'm sure you will understand and help me.... Dadi, I want to live with my husband. I don't want to live here in India, while he lives abroad, with someone else..."

Dadi's busy hands stilled at whatever they were doing. She looked into her niece's eyes. Understanding and sympathy crept in. Who else but Neel would know that pain?

"Yes, Neel, you'll live with him. I'll see to it." Her voice was firm and Neel was sure that since Dadi had said it, it would happen. How she did not know. Dadi had her ways and her tongue.

Neelima's cup was full when Dada flew down for her wedding. The only cloud was that he came alone. "It would have been lovely if – but never mind."

The engagement day dawned. It had been a whirl, shopping, planning, tailoring, and the works. Now the actual rituals were to start... in the good old way, an amalgam of so many types, *misri* and fruits, prayers and songs, a cake and a ring blessed by a *pundit*!

As soon as the rituals were over, someone, Neelima never figured out who suggested, "Neelima has a lovely voice. Ask her to sing."

The poor girl would have drowned in embarrassment as the chorus grew. The old faces grew negative, Vadi Amma, Ammi, Dadis, Ma, her in-laws – but the young people found support from unexpected quarters, her own father added his personal entreaties. Patting her on her back, he said, "Sing, *bete*, you have a gift from God. But don't give us a *bhajan* just now," he added ruefully.

Neelima looked around wildly. No *bhajan*, but no love song either at all those dour faces. What to sing? She stole a look at Hari. His hands were folded neatly over his crossed legs and he was staring straight ahead, fixedly, as if willing himself away from this place and its gaudy raucous populace.

"*Duniya mein hum aaye hain to jeena hi parega, jeevan hai agar zeher hai to peena hi parega...*" it was a depressing choice for an engagement party. Her cousins giggled conspicuously, but the dour older faces relaxed a little.

Neelima's first test came soon after marriage – to coax a smile from Hari and from his dour old father. Hari, she found, lived in mortal fear of his father whose nasty temper and ready use of his fists made all and sundry give him a wide berth. These and other horror stories only came tumbling out after the wedding was safely over. Apprehensive of the stories of broken bones and smashed crockery, Neelima kept herself firmly out of the old man's reach.

When they were due to leave, Neelima pestered Hari to take her out for a movie. "I have not seen Hindi movies for ages. Let's see all we can now."

"We've already seen two this week. Baba will get angry."

"We'll tell him later. Let's go," pleaded Neelima prettily.

When they got home, Dour Face was waiting. Neelima put on her pretty pleading face, but he look through her at his son.

"How dare you?" He landed a mighty slap on Hari's cheek. Neelima was aghast. As the bile rose, she gagged and threw up. She had never seen a grown man being slapped like this. Hari was a married man, her husband!

Tears welled up in Hari's eyes. There was no hiding his unmanning by his own father, that too in front of his bride. But where could he hide in this massive apartment crowded with people? Leaving the house was impossible with the old man keeping guard.

Hari's face was almost unrecognisable. It was not that the old Dour Face had a very heavy hand, rather it was the impact that mattered. Hari staggered into his room where Neelima was washing the vomit off her beautiful embroidered sari. Her heart went out to him. She dropped the *sari* into a corner and went to him.

Hari's face had crumbled to a 'pudding' consistency – his handsome visage became a mockery of itself. Neelima caught him as he collapsed on the bed and drew him to her, shocked to the core at the sight of a grown man crying. Sobs racked the slim frame as single words sputtered out; broken phrases and sentences reeled out the shameful story of a stunted life.

"I don't want to live. Is this life? Living in a constant fear? We thought he had changed after coming home to India and being with his mother and family. But he is just the same. I'm a man, a grown married man with a wife. Not a schoolboy to be thrashed. All his life, he has done this – beat, punch, slap, pinch, fists, cane, ruler, slippers – ma, the girls, me."

"Why didn't you leave him?"

"Where for? There was nowhere to go. We were abroad, in a foreign country. What will people say? Who will say what? All day it is work, work and go home. All day *bhajans* and *kirtan*. No going anywhere. Parties, he would go alone. He only took Ma out on Diwali, that's all. Yes, we had good clothes, good food, good, expensive schools, but always the rule was do not talk to anyone. Don't enjoy anything.

"In school at least, I had a few friends, but didn't know what to talk to them, what to say, what to hide. I used to bunk classes to sit alone in the library and read a book, or sit behind the trees to watch the squirrels and the birds and the sky. At home it was hell all the time, the shop was worse – that is why I purposely failed three times, just to delay having to go full time to the shop and be with him all day..."

Neelima's eyes popped. For all the cantankerousness of her relatives, they had never gone that far.

"After two whole years, he gave me the charge of taking supplies to the Las Palmas shop. Then charge of the Tangiers Operations. Now he is retired. I have to run the entire business. And he treats me like THIS!"

They had collapsed into the bed. Neelima pulled out her bottle of cream and smoothened Hari's face, massaging it lovingly as she listened to his tale. As her fingers worked their magic, she closed her eyes to stop the rush of tears washing away her dreams of a beautiful life in a foreign land. What beautiful life was this?

The night was almost over before they slept, exhausted by the storm that had made Neelima a woman overnight. She knew that she was responsible now, not just for herself, but also her husband. There was no question of any child until he grew up, out of the shadow of his father. Since Dour Face was now retired from the business, going away was the best thing to happen to both Hari and Neelima.

"Don't do or say anything. Just pretend nothing happened. First, we have to get away from here. Don't let anything stop or delay that," she pleaded with Hari. Cradling her husband in her arms, she swore, "I'll never come back here – not till the old man is dead and gone."

Tangiers was a revelation, an insight into Hari's life.

The house was a stylish apartment, abounding in marble pillars and figurines and statuettes, decorated in muted variegated shades of tangerine – the handiwork of a skilled interior designer.

It was meant to showcase the position and wealth of a director of the company – now retired. It did not in any way reflect the personality of that director, or of any of his family members. Hari was not comfortable there. It was the company's headquarters. He was comparatively junior there, but carried weight as his father's son. That gave no joy to Hari and he was quick to carry Neelima off to the South.

Casablanca, Neelima found, was a twin city, the Old City and the European one. The Old City was noisy, colourful and full of Life and the other elegant, sophisticated and modern.

The house itself was a proper Mediterranean sprawl, white, cool and low slung over several courtyard. Bright colours, thought Neelima, would make it quite cheerful, as she walked in.

Casablanca was also the city of Baba's alter ego. Hari had warned, "He is Baba's eyes and ears; sometimes his brain too, so be careful." Neelima was shocked by a face as dour, if not more than old Dour Face back home. At the first meeting, he said quite casually, "You've just arrived. Do not start housekeeping just yet. Drop in for dinner at my place tonight."

Neelima took the invitation at face value and accepted with a pretty smile. In the evening, she extracted a delicious blue chiffon *sari* with delicate lacy embroidery. When they arrived, she saw the number of cars parked in the driveway and was glad she had worn her pearl set with the embroidered chiffon *sari*.

The smile froze on her face and on Dour Face's when they entered. Her pretty blue lace and pearls were just not up to the competition from the heavy formal silks and *zardozis* dripping gold and diamonds gathered there.

It was past midnight when they reached home. The call from India came shortly after. A bleary-eyed Hari recoiled in shock. "*Naak kata di meri.* Why did I give your wife diamonds, rubies and emeralds if she wanted to wear only pearls at the welcome dinner…?"

The long distance posting ushered in their new life in Casablanca.

"What is wrong, Neel? Why no babies yet?" there was genuine concern in Maman's eyes. "Hari?"

"No Maman, I don't want babies. I can barely look after him yet. It's been over four years and I have yet to make him laugh." They both knew of Neelima's resolve, to make her husband laugh like she had seen her father laugh in Paris.

In all the years since her marriage, Neelima had been more in touch with Paris than with India. Now Neelima knew how her father had lived away from home for so long, yet not lost touch. Others gave him news, just as she herself got much more news in frequent letters from home, which made no mention of Paris at all. No one even knew of them.

It was Dada's support that had brought the visible changes in their Life. Hari began with the semi-weekly trips from Casablanca to keep the company shop in Las Palmas stocked and supervised. The Las Palmas group of islands was dense with holiday resorts, hotels, taverns and beaches frequented by free spending tourists, which made for rich pickings.

Neelima accompanied him on a couple of the trips and found life more congenial at Las Palmas, away from the Dour Face II.

"Hari, why don't we live in Las Palmas, rather than Casablanca?"

"Neelu, the company headquarters are there."

"So what? In any case you come here twice a week. Why not stay here and go there twice a week?"

"Can you see them allowing it? Allowing us to lead a life of our own without their breathing down our necks?"

"Let's try at least. If you stand firm, they can't stop you," Neelima encouraged.

It took some convincing. But soon, they had decided, against the stiff opposition, to shift base to Las Palmas and let Hari made semi-weekly trips to Casablanca.

At Las Palmas, Neelima's first venture was to cut up her numerous *saris* to turn out a range of stunning gowns, which was snapped up. When she wrote to Dadi to send her more *saris* in bulk, the parcel arrived at the Casablanca office and triggered off another long distance pasting.

"How many parties do you attend that your wife needs so many expensive *saris*? Does money grow on trees?"

It was Dada who arranged for the next consignment and Neelima flew to her Paris *maika* to collect it and catch up with the latest designs. Her gown sales were growing into an exclusive boutique in one of Las Palmas' bigger hotels. Dada and Maman flew down to celebrate. The celebration sprouted another spin-off, when Dada fell in love with a tiny tavern on a neighbouring island, Tenerife. The old man running it wanted to sell out.

"Let's buy it and run it. It's an expansion opportunity…"

"But, Baba…" stuttered Hari.

Everything was swept aside by Dada and Maman's enthusiasm.

"I'll buy it, Neelima will run it, and it will not be part of Baba's empire. It will be your own." Neelima turned hotelier and shuttled between Tenerife, Las Palmas and sometimes Casablanca. Hari constantly lived in fear of being discovered, since they had not announced the Tenerife venture. Neelima too lived in fear, but she had to cover up her fears to shore up Hari's courage.

"What can he do? He is not coming here. We can put down the phone when he starts shouting. If he disowns us, so much the better," she concluded.

In her heart of hearts, she knew of Hari's dependence on the hardness of his father and on his mother's softness too.

"Look, Neel," Maman brought her out of her reverie, "Looking after Hari so much won't work. He is a man. Let him be one. He has to accept responsibility. Put that responsibility, of caring for his own offspring, on him – it may yet make a man of him."

"Maman, I have not yet made him laugh."

"All the more reason for you to do so. Once he has responsibility of being a father, he can get out of his father's shadow and be his own man. Then only can he live his own life. It is not for all to become your papa and laugh at life so openly and enjoy it too."

That was true. Dada was the only man Neelima had seen laughing such a wholesome laugh, despite the blights on his life, the family rancour, Bhagwanti who always made him feel guilty, Vasudev his younger brother who refused to talk to him because he had a foreign wife, Mahesh, his son, Neelima's younger brother who hated him.

How often, in the run up to her marriage, Mahesh had railed against his father, taunting Neelima for her open admiration of her father. "How can you correspond with that man? Who is he? Is he ever there for us, for our mother? He is only there for his foreign keep..."

Neelima wanted to lash out at him. However, prudence stilled her tongue. Dada had warned her against getting involved in any verbal duels over Maman. "Neel, Maman will not benefit and your mother will get hurt thinking you have gone against her. Since we do not hear them, their words cannot touch us or hurt us. So don't make any issue of what anyone says…"

Little did anyone know that a few years later, Shyam would be sending Rose to meet Ammi and Maya face-to-face?

As it turned out, the arrival of the babies was momentous. After months of casting aspersions over the delay, the announcement of her pregnancy was cause for an international jubilation, be it Las Palmas, Morocco, Paris or India.

Her refusal to leave Tenerife was cause for consternation. "Thousands of women have their babies here. Why cannot I?" declared Neelima stoutly.

Finally Hari announced that he was handing over the courier duties to someone else, to take charge of the entire Las Palmas operations, the tavern at Tenerife, Neelima's boutique and the company shop in Las Palmas itself. For once in his life, Hari stood up to his Baba. He took the joy out of the old man's celebrations on becoming a grandfather, by becoming a Man himself.

In vain, did Baba burn the international trunk lines and even called out his storm trooper, Dour Face II. "Casablanca and Tangiers are a very big operation, several times the Las Palmas ones. What is this little hotel business? Holiday home for cheap tourists? Piffle – *naak cut jayegi*." But nothing of his accusations moved the stolid Hari.

"We'll eat less but we'll eat our own food – not beholden to anyone."

Finally, the old people had to back down – rather gracelessly. Nevertheless, they insisted on leaving Hari in charge of the Las Palmas operations – after all, he was Baba's son and the company's prestige would take a knock if he walked out of it. Dour Face II even offered to take over the tavern. When Hari refused, he drew up plans for another company shop alongside it, to shore up sales.

Hari was on a rare high. He actually smiled without reason. "Maybe the laugh will come soon," mused Neelima as she wove dreams of the impending arrival of her first baby.

Saloni was followed quickly by the twins, Nina and Nikita. No one used their *kundli* names. Their pet names finally gave away Neelima's secret to her mother, that she was in constant touch with her father and his French wife. Dadi wrote regularly, passing on all the family news, Mahesh rarely, if at all. He was working as far away as possible in distant Panama.

As the girls grew and business flourished, the old people longed to see the granddaughters. However, Hari and Neelima made no plans for a trip to India. Hari's sister Sarla was to get married and Hari would have to go. However, Neelima was adamant. The clash burnt up the long distance wires. Finally Dour Face II came to argue Baba's case.

"How can I take these little babies? It would be cruel. First all those weather changes, from here to London and then Bombay, then an overcrowded wedding."

"You are the eldest bhabhi. It is your duty."

"Hari is going. He'll do whatever is to be done."

"You have to go with him. It will look very bad if you do not go."

"What if the babies fall ill and all that? Who will look after them, if I am running the *shaadi*? My duty lies with them until they are a little older."

"There are plenty of ladies to help you out at home."

"Let them look after the *shaadi* then." The ding-dong battle went on all day.

"Your father-in-law wants all of you there for the wedding. You haven't been home once in all these years since your wedding. Don't you realise that if Hari goes alone, people will talk? Maybe they'll corner him and turn him against you? Even marry him off elsewhere? Where'll you be then, Neelima?"

Ah hah, now the gloves were off. Neelima was not too sure that it was just a piece of rhetoric. There was just that much anguish on the old man's face to make her pause and turn over what he blurted out at long last.

"Would the old man go so far as to re-impose his will on his son?"

For almost ten years, Neelima had avoided a home visit, despite all the bluster, the demands and business changes. Now?

Neelima squared her shoulders as she looked at the old man in the eye. "Hari is not a child. He will definitely go to fulfil his duty to his sister. In addition, if Baba wants to force another marriage on him, don't forget, Hari is no spring chicken to be caught and deplumed. My relatives are there too to see what goes on. Hari is a man, a husband and a father. Don't you think he too knows his duties to his wife and daughters? If he has to succumb to his father's blackmail, and be resold in the dowry market, better he goes out of our lives before his daughters learn to recognise him as their father." The threat was implicit. It broke Dour Face II's armour.

The joy had, in any case, gone out of Hari's home trip. Going there alone? To face Baba's wrath? Ma's carping? Hordes of relatives asking after Neelima and the girls?

His wife put on her 'cheerful motherly' face. "Look at the brighter side. You'll see everyone. Show them the photographs. Exaggerate their health problems, teething, fever, measles, what not. And if they offer you another bride, tell her, she'll have to be the babies' 'new ayah'." The tone was light but her eyes were serious. Hari looked straight into them as he folded her into his arms.

"I'll not let you down, Neel. He is my father. And I am their father. Besides, don't I know, you'll chase me down to Kingdom come and bring me back?" he ended gaily.

Hari's tickets were booked through to India and back. There were tense moments, both in India and for Neelima. The ten days were prolonged agony as Neelima's distracted mind played out various scenarios, all dramatic, all teetering to disaster. Hari's call confirmed all her worst fears over an ugly filial clash.

On the third day, when Maman flew in to hold her hands, she found a pale distraught Neelima, bordering on a breakdown. Once against the long distance wires crackled – Las Palmas to Paris, from Paris to India. This time it was Dada who went to the Big House to call out his storm troopers, Dadi, Bhagwanti and his bhabhis, to shore up Hari's defences.

Dadi in full form was a formidable redoubt – even a Dour Face dare not overstep the line with Dadi around. The old lady knew how to be charming when she wanted to be. Neither sugar nor butter would melt in her mouth.

"Baba, why are you worried? We'll take care of everything. Haven't I gotten so many daughters married off in all these years? *Betiyaan to sab ki hoti hain.* What do young people know about organising a marriage? Let them just enjoy themselves."

She sent off Hari with some young cousins to distribute cards while she bustled around, setting the trousseau out to see what remained to be bought, organising its fancy packing, checking the menus and the giveaways to various relatives.

With Dadi's presence in the house all day, Baba was forced to check his tongue. Not only that, in a vain glory effort to show off in front of a *samdhan*, one from the Big House at that, he was extra lavish with the giveaways and trinkets, even the trousseau and its decoration. For this, Sarla was eternally grateful to Dadi. She quietly hugged the old woman, "You have saved all our lives and made mine. Otherwise, Baba's *kanjoosi* would have made me the laughing stock of my *sasural*. Perhaps it is good that bhabhi didn't come for the wedding, so you could come. How can I ever thank you enough?"

*****

6

NO. 7

Among the beautiful white clad drones, there was one stark figure, one who would have given Maya a run for her money with an emaciated face; her visage was distinctly bitter and spiteful or perhaps scornful? Who was she? And what was she doing here looking so scornful, so jealous and so sorrowful all at the same time?

Gayatri's cup of woe was full to the brim. She was the sole survivor of her family. There were many to declare that she was on the verge of insanity. If she held back at the brink, or occasionally came back, it was only thanks to the ever-faithful Shakubai, ever-ready raconteur, droning out her tragic tale about House No. 7 in the old *Bazaar*.

*****

It is difficult to imagine a narrower house, squeezed in between equally narrow ones, all in a row... the precursors of modern Row Houses, no doubt.

Occasionally, one saw a broader one in the row of balconies, obviously someone had made good, but did not want to move out of the neighborhood; instead that someone had bought out a neighbour or two to make a broader, grander house.

The tiny balconies overlooked a narrow, bustling *Bazaar*, yet to make the grade to a modern 'Shopping Complex'. The balconies were set well back from the front of the shops, no dropping garbage into the shop-front street.

All were at least three-tiered, the upper ones set even further back, apparently just the appurtenances to a tiny *barsati*, with a tinier patch open to the sky for someone to stand and breathe fresher air up there.

The architecture was distinctly turn-of-the-century, the tall ceilings and the adjoining residences kept the narrow houses cool with no inlet for the sun, except an occasional skylight. Ventilation was strictly back to front, limited by the *Bazaar* in front and a narrower lane with another identical set of row houses at the back.

Despite the enclosed atmosphere, it was not a trap; rather it was a safe haven of sorts for many, including the denizens of No.7.

Or was it? Opinions differ.

Few shoppers ever glanced up, and if any did, none would have noted the three sentinels, Laurel and Hardy feminised on the balcony over No.7 and the Witch above them, gazing malevolently down at her nieces below.

Laurel and Hardy were actually Dammi and Gayatri, and the Witch was their father's sister, Phuphi. No one remembered her name, they only called her Phuphi. Phuphi and their father Purshottam were the children of Amma's youngest brother-in-law who had shifted his family out of the Big House in a fit of pique soon after the Partition. But obviously the family connection could never be completely broken, could it?

Dammi was slender, as adolescence had thinned out her spare frame. Delicate built, her high-cheek bones and long hair gave her an ethereal look at the time of her marriage. Over the years, life coarsened her texture, her eyes narrowed almost permanently; a sneer upset the symmetry of her Cupid lips.

As for Gayatri, the roly-poly little girl had grown into a voluptuous beauty who astounded the neighbours with her bouts of thinness. Did she starve, they often thought. With age, the voluptuousness fermented into an over-blown rose, loose of flesh, limb, and eye.

Neighbours often wondered at the tomb-like silence of No.7. Did they never speak? Or only in whispers? No one recalled hearing sounds of normal conversation from there. Shakubai was the do-it-all maidservant of several houses and acknowledged mistress of No.7.

"Listen," she had started off, for all the world like a *kathakar* of old, "They were three, two sisters and a brother, the two beautiful *Apsaras* and he handsome as a God.

"The elder sister never married. Now she is in and out of mental asylums. I go to see her there at times. All her life, she kept herself covered from top to toe, covering her head with a *dupatta* all day long and preaching against sex; Phuphi taught her nieces to fear sex, constantly reminding them about its disastrous effects. Now there are days when she keeps tearing up her clothes to walk around stark naked and drives the *pagalkhanawallahs* quite crazy keeping up with her."

"WHY?" That will come later. "First, her younger sister fell in love, but Purshottam Dada did not approve of the boy. He did not belong to their caste. He beat up his little sister to an inch of her life. When he spoke of an engagement with someone else, she consumed poison.

"Then Brother-Dear got married and *Hey, Ram*, morning, noon or night, totally *besharam*, calling his wife to bed, with an unmarried sister and mother in such a small house. He was totally callous even to his wife's health. No wonder the elder one took such a dislike to marriage and all it entails. Shame killed his mother.

"Whenever he came home from his *pardesi* job, for at least five-six months at a time, the wife would have one or two miscarriages, but he never stopped or changed his ways. The poor woman died after giving him the son he wanted above all else, never bothered about his two daughters. Who does anyway?

"In no time at all, he had remarried and soon after, got the two little girls married off and took his wife and the boy *pardes* with him.

"He has never come back; it is over a decade now. *Ram jaane* whether the second wife is still alive, she was also a pretty little thing, but not too sturdy and he could not have changed his ways. His only good point was that he has never failed to send the money."

There was a sharp reaction at the mention of filthy lucre. "What money?"

"Money for those left behind, mother, sister, and daughters and now even me to look after the house and maintain it, keep it clean, whitewash every year, paint every other year, even though he has never returned. Who knows the son may come some day to get married?"

"But what happened to the daughters and the sister, the Phuphi in the *pagalkhana*?"

"For years and years, after their marriages, neither Gayatri nor Dammi came home. For what? What was there to come home too? The mother was dead and gone and only Phuphi was there. She had given them the direst warnings against marriage; how could they face her and adjust to the senility which had overcome her with age? Extremely cantankerous too.

"She used to drive everyone crazy with her superstitions and fasts; twenty days a month she would be fasting for something or the other.

"She lived in fear of *bhoots* and polluted shadows. If anyone's 'polluted' shadow fell on her *chulha* during that time of the month, she would discard the *chulha* and order a new one, happily fasting till it was installed. Shadows, *chhua-chhut* and hassles during menstruation were enough to drive anyone, even herself crazy. But came a time when the girls had to come. After all, such as it was, it was their home."

Shakubai recalled, "Gayatri's husband died when her son was scarce out of her womb. She had inherited her father's nature and to this day, her Sasuma insists *'Woh mere bete ko kha gayi'*. Gayatri could never have enough of him. Between that and drinking, TB claimed his life.

"Our Gayatri was a nice plump thing, but within a fortnight of his death, when I went to her *sasural*, she was thin as a reed. Starving. That old bitch just would not let her eat, just work, work all day. She let her servants go and made her slog."

Shakubai paused for breath and peered into her memories.

"One day," the *kathakar* continued, "her *Devar* returned. She used to tell me that it was like *jadu tona*. He had just to look and she would melt."

******

Gayatri had told Shakubai in confidence, "The first day he came home, he just looked at me and I felt as if I had been stripped. I was shaking and scared, not knowing what was to happen. You know, a few weeks before, my Sasu had been gossiping with the neighbours while I was washing the vessels. They were talking about a *'chaddar-charana'* and everyone had made queries about me.

"Sasu told me to look after him and I gave him dinner. He used to go out, and come home late. The next day he was out all day and came home just as we were going to bed. That night, he raped me in my *khatiya* right there in the courtyard with his mother a few yards away. I dared not make a sound, but Shakubai, my body betrayed me. It was even worse when he followed me to the little wood near the garden, where anyone could have come upon us."

"With that threat hanging over her head, Gayatri preferred to go to him when he decided to sleep in his father's room upstairs, that she had cleaned out, aired and scented for him. One night, she said, she spied her mother-in-law peeking through the ventilator. The next day, she was extra stingy, leaving her hungry."

"Perhaps," Shakubai recalled, "it was the hunger and the empty hope of a remarriage that captured Gayatri, I don't know, but the poor naive fool became addicted even to their beatings whenever the mother created trouble. She was reduced to a slut for his use during his holidays and his mother's slave otherwise. It took Gayatri years, she told me, to understand what sparked off this beating."

"Shakubai," Gayatri had explained plaintively, "He would be as sweet as honey; even refusing to believe his mother when she tried to make up a tale about anything. And then suddenly, he would let fly. Much, much later, I realised that whenever I said that I was hungry, the word 'hungry' triggered off his fists. It was like magic, one minute he would be feeding me *jalebis* with his hands and the next, beating me to pulp because I said hungry."

"Mother and son used her terribly," moaned the faithful servant, "Unless you saw it for yourself, it is difficult to believe her condition. She would come home, thin as a reed, bruised, broken and bleeding, sometimes even with burn marks.

"The *vaid* told me that a *dai* had emptied her womb just before she was sent home, almost bleeding to death. Sometimes, I cursed the *vaid* for making her hale and hearty again. I would massage her bruised body, oil her hair and face and feed her up and within weeks, she would her plump self. She had amazing recouping powers, her laughing eyes would smile and her giggle would be loud, but with them would come the quickening of her other senses and then he would come, her *Devar*.

"And no matter how much she would have railed against him when she had arrived, and swore never to return to her *sasural*, as soon as he came, giving her the glad eye and put before her some silly trinket on a basket of *jalebis* and her favourite *kachouris*, she would be itching to go back with him to the *sasural*. Nothing to keep her here except the silent witch.

"Lord knows what it was there, I have never seen anybody become that thin working at home, but when she came back again, bruised and bleeding, she would be as thin as a reed. In later years, she used to go back not plump but fat, even gross, because as long as she was home, all she did was eat, eat, eat all the time munching like a goat... and that is what Dammi could not stand about her.

"The last time she came, Dammi had also come home. The two prickled at each other because Gayatri was used to having the house to herself and now her place had to be shared with Dammi who was Phuphi's obvious favourite too. Over the weeks, the vibes between the two grew increasingly strained, as if though unspoken, their habits had begun to clash and grit at each other.

"Dammi stubbornly fended off all queries about her abrupt return home with pointed sarcasm at the other's eating bouts and her growing size. Both ate healthily but while Gayatri ballooned out, her face and limbs filling out visibly, Dammi remained as she was, thin as a reed, a volcano of nervous energy.

"She embarked on a thorough spring clean of the house, discarding piles of accumulated junk which the Phuphi would never let me throw out. She got the house whitewashed, even called the plumber and masons for long pending repairs. Then she started to stitch new fresh white *mulmul* curtains for the windows from the old lady's stock of white *dupattas*.

"If Gayatri ever wondered why she herself had never thought of doing all that, she never mentioned it. All she did was poke and prod about why Dammi had suddenly appeared out of the blue. It was like speaking to a blank wall.

"How that dam burst or why, I don't know. One day as I was finishing the washing up, I heard Dammi speaking..."

"He beat me... all the time, he beat me, with his hands, his shoes, his *lathi*, anything. He was an animal in his violence and his callousness. For some time he had been *shagird* at some *akhada* and knew how to punish without leaving any evidence, but oh, how he used to beat me," Dammi wailed low and long.

"Money, he often spent like water, but with an underlying tinge of meanness. Every day, he would buy colourful glass bangles on his way to visit his mistress, and he would bring the discarded ones of yesterday for his wife. Why spend twice the money every day, he reasoned. When I came to know of it, I refused to wear them, then he would beat me up and force them on my wrists. When I struggled, he started to deliberately smash my wrists against the wall, like they do for widows, until some of the glass cut my wrists."

It was difficult to understand why Dammi's husband, the Walrus-moustachioed one, with a chirpy, buxom mistress, beat up his emaciated wife. Was it because her thinness was no compliment to him as a provider? There was no dearth of provisions in the house – meat, fruit, sweets – everything went into the kitchens in generous measure. "She ate well enough," he often thought. Yet she remained painfully thin. People had asked pointed questions sometimes. So he used to beat her.

Then years began to slip by without her conceiving. He used to beat her perhaps because she not only did not produce a legitimate heir; she hadn't even produced a female proof of his manhood!

How long and how often he had heaved over her and at her. Tried all the aphrodisiacs recommended by the *hakims*, the *vaid*, and the cheeky friends. But not once did she even miss a period, not even for a couple of weeks to offer some glimmer of hope.

"*Banjh*," he flung at her as he slung out. And Dammi just stood blankly taking the punishment, her eyes contemptuously stoic in their baleful glare.

Often he would beat her because she failed to respond to his lovemaking. How often he had compared the difference in the responses of his two women, the one so wantonly pleasurable and the other so cold and unpleased.

Obviously Dammi was only fulfilling a duty. Unable or unwilling to enjoy it or let him enjoy it. Maybe, just maybe, he sometimes pondered, a jot of enjoyment or pleasure would ensure some fruition, which evaded them.

He would rise furious and begin to lash out at her verbally and physically. But she had become immune to the beating. Sex held no charm for her, after all the dire warnings of her Phuphi against That Sin of Man – a sin that, childhood memories and Phuphi's preaching warned, had carried away her mother from the ministrations of her over-sexed father.

Whenever he came home for his prolonged holiday, she recalled quite clearly, he would call out to her any time, morning, noon or night and Phuphi's mutterings would start, "Heathen, devil, lout, and destroyer, sapping her life."

The dire prediction proved true. The mother had died in her prime. Within months, the father remarried. He had married off both his daughters in haste and took off with his bride and little son, leaving Phuphi alone in the narrow house above the *Bazaar*.

Apart from Phuphi's warnings and the sheer physical pain, maybe she could not accept him because of her. On the way home after the wedding, Dammi had learnt that he already had a mistress. His relatives were so proud that 'he could afford a keep – they are expensive, you know, only silk clothes, *attar* and jewels...' they had twittered behind her back maliciously, wanting her to hear and feel hurt.

They only reason, they said, why the mistress was not also the lady of the house and mother of his child, was because of her antecedents. So Dammi's bounden duty, why she had been brought into the house, was to produce an heir.

It froze her insides and rendered her, perhaps equally impotent to his skilful lovemaking, always that freezing, nagging thought "Had she taught him how to do this?"

"One day in the *bazaar*," Dammi recounted, "I spied a lovely *kada* at the goldsmith's where we had stopped. I asked the price and wanted to examine the filigree work more closely. My husband was furious."

"Where do you think money comes from?" he shouted standing there in the middle of the *bazaar*.

"A few minutes earlier, I had seen him pass money surreptitiously after Lala's assistant had handed over a box to a pretty buxom woman. Their sly looks told me who she was and now it was my turn. I took off my *kada*. You know the one, remember that pair of Ma's which Dada gave us one each, which had a twisted dragon head from China with jewelled eyes, yours had rubies and mine emeralds. I put the *kada* on Lalaji's little table and told him loudly to make me the filigree one of equal weight, size and cost. The look on his face was worth the thrashing I got when we got home. But the *kada* was not sent home. One day I went to collect it. Lalaji said my husband had collected it and just then, she walked past, flaunting my *kada* in my face."

Three gasps resounded in the narrow house, one from upstairs, one across the table and one from behind the kitchen door.

"What could I do? I killed the damned bitch. Why do you think I came home?" exclaimed Dammi with exasperation at their lack of understanding.

After that fateful confession, no cajoling could extract anything more from her, no entreaties, no wails, no threats, nothing. It was back to the Tomb of Silence with the non-stop Muttering from upstairs, only now the muttering had an unexpectedly light tone, as if the witch was pleased that at least one of the girls had done her proud!

One day, there was a great commotion in the *Bazaar*. *Pardes se police aayi hai.* The wild whisper spread like fire, scurrying through the long market and its upper floor denizens, how no one knew.

In the Tomb of Silence, obviously, no one did know, they were staring at their respective patches of wall or ceiling, unconscious of the impending doom.

The police van had stopped importantly at a crossroad before the market narrowed dangerously. Important-looking policemen in starched uniforms stepped down quite self-consciously and pulled down a bound prisoner, bulky, dusty and dishevelled, hands tied behind his back with a rope and walrus-moustache quivering as he argued his innocence and cajoled, "Let's go, let's go, I'll show you the murderess."

They marched down the *Bazaar* into the tiny lane, pushed open the back door smartly up the stairs at No.7. The Witch peeped as usual from her eerie corner of the upper floor at the noisy entrants.

As soon as the door opened, Walrus burst out, "There she is, that bitch, there she is. Look, look at her, inspector *sahib*, look at the audacity of her, standing there so boldly meeting our eyes without even covering her head, cold-hearted murderess... she is the one, I tell you, she..."

His tone turned desperate at the impassiveness on the face of the police officer, matched by the impassive bold stare of his thin wife.

"Say something, damn you, say something." He tried but couldn't flail his tied arms. "Didn't you give me that box of poisoned *pedas*, so innocently, inspector *sahib*, so innocently she sat on the bed, putting one in her mouth and taunted me about my keep, she said," he swallowed, "she said take the rest to her, don't take this one out of my mouth, like... like... like..." the accusing voice faltered.

"Like?" prompted the policeman, "Like what?"

"Like you took away my mother's gold *kada* for your *randi*," finished a cold feminine voice. "What have you come here for, now, after robbing me blind?"

The policeman pounced. "What did he rob you off?"

"My mother's gold *kada* tor his keep."

"And you sent her poisoned *pedas*?"

"No question of them being poisoned. I ate one from the box in front of him, even he ate one, gobbled it in fact, ask him."

"You picked it out and gave it to him?"

"Yes, along with the rest of the packet." Hats off for sheer bravado!

"Bibiji," the policeman was solemn in his pronouncement, "After the poisoning, he had run away, but we caught up with him and now he has led us to you. We have proof that it was you who bought the poison. You are now under arrest."

If he had hoped for an explosion, for some reaction from his stoic wife, Walrus was severely disappointed. Dammi stood stock still for a while. Then her eyes narrowed at the gross, sweating figure of her wheezing husband. She turned to the self-consciously starched figure of the Inspector.

"I will say my good-byes," and marched stiffly upstairs. Speechlessly a constable took position at the bottom of the stairs, eyes firmly up. Not a word was spoken as aunt and niece embraced, then drew back to gaze deep into each other's eyes.

The younger woman was looking intently over her aunt's shoulder. The old woman turned to follow her gaze to the point in her kitchen where tools were arraigned against the wall and then again looked deep into her niece's eyes, as if in acknowledgement.... Was there a tinge of pride?

The Inspector cleared his throat audibly and promptly Dammi came down the stairs, barely acknowledging the piteous wails of her fat sister.

"I am ready." The voice was firm, the face stoic and the eyes glistening.

As they reached the first narrow steps, a frail quavering voice was heard coming from up stairs, "Daughter, you've left this behind."

All motions paused as eyes turned up wondering what it was Dammi had left behind when she had not taken a thing with her. A wicked chuckle accompanied a loud thud crashing down.

Swift as a flash, the Thin One pulled Walrus towards her and shoved his thick head into the stairwell. Before anyone could stop it, the grinding stone had splattered his brains on the wall opposite before crashing down in smithereens.

Triumphantly lunatic laughter ricocheted through the eerie awed silence.

*****

7

LAAJJO

A very attractive Juno, tall, slim and well preserved, the white setting off her wheatish complexion sat next to Dadi at the funeral. There were those who looked askance at her presence in the family gathering.

Perhaps it was that latent hostility, more felt than seen which drew her close to Dadi's ample person with that austere look and the dour face which had remained just so for decades. Careworn hands bore evidence to the labour of the beautician which failed to impart any elegance of even the most rudimentary order. Dadi's white cottons had long since been replaced by the elegant soft whites. It was Dadi perhaps who was most affected by Maya's going.

Laajjo was the spoil brat of the family, spoilt childishly by her mother, right under the noses of the disapproving grandma's and all.

"So what if you are one year older than me. I'm your husband's sister. You should call me Didi."

Bullying came naturally to Laajjo and this started within hours of bringing home Sunita, her new bhabhi. Sunil, the groom balefully temporised, "You'll not become smaller by calling her Didi. So what if there is a few months difference between you."

The next argument happened on the breakfast table a few days later.

"Sunita, I don't want eggs and bread. Make me a *paratha*," Laajjo fumed at the breakfast table.

The new bride looked around. The *mehendi* was yet on her hands. She had been told to stay out of the kitchen at least till it faded.

"Go on, you'll not become smaller by making something for your husband's sister," said her mother-in-law, Parvati.

And so it went on. Hubbie dear only wanted peace but Laajjo and her mother wanted service. Sunita saw relief only when Laajjo was married off. Her heart lightened as Laajjo's wedding ceremonies progressed. First came the engagements, first *kachhi* and then the *pucci* one with *misri* and *tokras* of fruits, fresh and dry, and the party to go with it. Then came the pre-nuptial *sagri*, when her prospective in-laws trooped in with beautiful floral ornaments, *tikka*, earrings, necklace, bracelets, toe rings, anklets, the works, each representing the gold and diamonds ones which would be presented to her at the wedding.

Then came the *mehendi* and the *sangeet* and then the *navgrahi*, to appease all the nine planets and the seven *suhagans* participating in the grinding ritual to introduce the bride to household duties. Finally, the actual marriage with the vast trousseau and all the razzle-dazzle that the family could rustle up.

"Deliverance is at hand," Sunita gloated silently.

Alas! The deliverance did not last. Four days after her marriage, Laajjo reached home in floods of tears.

"Ma, nobody loves me. Nobody gives me what I want. I have to give them what they want."

"What happened?"

"I said I want *aaloo roti* and they said, get up and make some for yourself and for all of us too."

"Who said that? I'd told them you cannot cook."

"His sisters."

"How dare they!"

"Doesn't your husband say anything?" asked her cousins.

"He says that I won't become smaller by learning everything from sisters…"

"Why do you take all that rot?" they asked.

"They speak so sweetly. How to say 'no' without sounding like a vamp?" pondered Laajjo.

"*Dimaag kharab ho gaya hai un logon ka,*" decreed her mother with asperity.

Dadi poured cold water on the brewing crisis.

"Look Laajjo, here your bhabhi waited on you. Now you have to do the same in your *sasural* for your husband's sisters. And behave yourself. Now you are a married woman and you are bound to uphold the honour of both the families, not to create battles between them. If they are sweet, you become sweeter, until you learn to become a sweet poison. Till then, be sweet and don't you dare spoil our family name," she ended pitilessly.

Despite Dadi's stern warning, the peace did not last. It could not. And Laajjo's weeping visits became a regular feature. Till they reached a crescendo.

"Now you have to do something. Save me. Do something. I'll die there," she declared dramatically as she stepped into the house.

"Now what?"

"He's not going to Hong Kong but to the States."

"So what? America offers better prospects."

"Why don't you understand? Hong Kong visas are easy to get. I could go along with him. But if he goes to the US, he'll go alone and I'll be stuck here between the devil and the deep blue sea. If and when I do go to the States, I'll have to work. There are no servants there. Here too I'm a slave."

Dadi intervened brusquely. "What rubbish! They have a cook and a part-time servant. Does supervising servants also called slavery?"

"No. I'm slave to my sisters-in-law. Both are social worker types. They want to cart me off with them every day. First *papad* making in Pimpri left my hands swollen, then it was distributing fruits in hospitals and slums and then the bloody Ladies Club. They don't even play cards. I'll die of boredom and good works."

Sunita turned away to hide her smile as the others closed in on Laajjo. Now life was giving Laajjo what she used to hand out.

Tragedy struck soon though. After a painful three year stint with Lata and Rita's social work, Laajjo finally got her US visa. Less than six weeks later, she was back, this time draped in white.

Her husband had fallen to a stray passing shot from a car full of boisterous youngsters. It was deemed best for a tourist-visa-holder-wife of an illegal immigrant to leave at the earliest.

Even before the family rallied round, Laajjo was enfolded in her *sasural's* embrace. She was pregnant and neither her mother-in-law nor her sisters-in-law would let her out of their sight. They even accompanied her to her *maika*.

"How can we leave her alone, in this condition? You know, a woman's moods in pregnancy get reflected in the child. Remember Abhimanyu in the *Mahabharata*. We cannot allow her to sit alone and brood. It will harm the child. Empty hands are the Devil's workshop."

And so it came about that finally Laajjo learnt to do all the things she had never learnt at home, which included cooking, making pickles, sewing and crochet, visiting schools and slums, acting like a Gracious Lady.

"I want to scream and shout," she confided to her cousins at the Big House.

"Why?"

"All day, do this, do that, be good. How can anyone be good all the time? These people will definitely drive me crazy."

"Hold on. They'll probably stop all this when the baby comes."

That prophecy was fulfilled. All the good works stopped. But a new, equally tedious routine started. Laajjo found herself surrounded by the baby talk. nappies and feeds, till she had them coming out of her ears. Her only break was on her weekly visit home when she kept the baby on Sunita's lap and relaxed herself.

"Take him out of my sight," she would demand, "I can't stand this baby all day. Ma, do something."

At which Dadi would reply by saying, "Is he yours or a borrowed one? Why can't you stand him? What do you expect us to do? Stay in your *sasural* to look after him?"

Parvati signalled her daughter to silence. In the quiet of her own room, she suggested, "Why don't you pay your servant a bit extra to wash his clothes and look after him?"

"Where's the money? And if I get caught…?"

"Don't worry. I'll arrange it."

"What?"

"I'll send our Gangubai there with some fruits. You just tell your Tarabai to give her a cup of tea."

"What'll you do?"

"Simple. I'll send fifty rupees and Tara will get her instructions.. Just wait and see."

It worked out beautifully. No one in the household could figure out why Tarabai was suddenly so solicitous of both Sonu and his mother.

But Laajjo's test was yet to come. One day, her father-in-law collapsed. He was hospitalised, and of course, everyone came calling. Laajjo's mother-in-law, Damayanti shrewdly chose Dadi's visit to bring up the issue of nursing.

"What to do? Both Rita and Lata are so busy with their duties. And I can hardly walk about. Someone has to be in the hospital with him all the time. One cannot trust these nurses and *ayahs*, no? We all have to take turns. It will mean the girls sacrificing their other duties…."

Dadi rose to the bait.

"Not at all. Why should they? What are bahus for? Laajjo will stay in the hospital and Lata and Rita can take turns at replacing her."

"What about my Sonu?" piped in Laajjo nervously, holding up her son.

"Don't worry, Laajjo, we'll look after him. In any case, he is so used to Tarabai, so that there will be no trouble at all." With a steely-eyed Dadi looking on sternly, Laajjo had no option but to bear it.

It was a difficult burden for her to put up with. The old man's gaunt frame weighed a ton. His breath smelt and so did his body fluids. Laajjo had to collect his cough and phlegm in a spittoon, but she drew the line at the bedpan... her face, sweet as sugar when guests poured in every evening and nasty as hell with the maids, raised many eyebrows in the hospital. News of this did trickle out finally to the Big House and to her sisters-in-law, Lata and Rita. But they did not say a word.

Things did finally change for Laajjo, when her father-in-law expired and her two sisters-in-law got married. It was for that occasion that Damayanti herself presented Laajjo with a pastel coloured *sari*.

"You have worn whites long enough," she said, "I don't want the white to become your prison."

Then Laajjo's wings began to sprout. But her sufferings had made her wiser, as she treaded warily. Marriage may have taken Lata and Rita out of the house, but for the time being, their visits to home were as frequent as Laajjo's had been to her own *maika*. And they had the advantage of Laajjo. Both her bhabhis had gone to their respective husbands in Panama and South Africa. She no longer had anyone to boss over. There were only cousins who could share her grief and not play slave to her. Laajjo learnt to be more diplomatic.

At a Ladies Club meet attended with Lata and Rita, she hung back and quietly left to stroll through the club, sizing up the situation. "Ammi," she addressed her mother-in-law in the presence of the sisters, "I'm getting fat and lethargic. There's a badminton court at the club. May I join it? I used to play badminton at school. There is yoga and sometimes *satsangs* too, if you want to come."

That was more than half the battle won with universal approval and in no time at all, Laajjo acquired a brand new wardrobe of *churidars* and *kurtas* in an array of soft colours for her badminton sessions and a range of exquisitely embroidered *saris* which were to become a Laajjo trademark. She shrewdly remained on the right side of the unspoken colour code, which included no reds or pinks for a widow. With her dusky complexion who needed them anyway? She evolved into a picture of cool elegance, despite her dusky looks.

Laajjo haunted the club, eager to talk to anyone, except her in-laws. At home, she ruled over the smallest issues.

"Black and white, what is this nonsense?" she burst out one day.

"What do you mean?"

"The old woman wants a colour TV in her room to watch her *bhajans* and yoga. Her daughters have colour TVs in their own homes. All my bhabhis have colour TVs in their homes. Even you have a colour TV here. Only I have to have a black and white one."

"Who said so?"

"Who else? When I said I wanted a TV in my room, they dumped their old black and white one on me."

"Why make an issue of it? It'll change sooner or later," reasoned Dadi.

"Why must I always wait? Only I? Why can't I have a colour TV? Because I am a widow?" she added slyly, touching off a raw nerve. The reaction it drew taught her a lesson forever on how to position herself in all the future battles.

For it was Dadi who flared up. "How dare they? Who says that the widows should only watch black and white TV? I'll get a new one…"

"No, no, why should you? They should get me one," the tension simmered; and neither Lata, nor Rita nor their mother ever knew how they were bamboozled into buying a brand new colour TV for Laajjo's exclusive use, by stinging remarks about how the world should change its attitude towards the widows. Coming from a senior family member like Dadi, who not only handled the family purse strings, but also had long years of widowhood behind her, there was no way that anyone could oppose what she said about the changing attitudes towards the widows.

Laajjo pushed the envelope further. Lata and Rita followed each other to their new homes in the foreign lands within months of each other. Her mother-in-law's aloneness was a boon for her.

"Now I have all that I want. For so many years the three of them ruled me. Now I am free," Laajjo raved and ranted when she went home to the Big House.

"Free from what?" asked Dadi sternly. Laajjo did not deign to answer, but exchanged knowing looks with her mother. Soon Laajjo's new-found freedom was evident to all, within the family circle, her in laws' circle and at the Club. She graduated from the badminton courts to the card room and the swimming pool and then the dance floor after becoming a fixture on the kitty and card party circuits.

She was also smart enough to ensure that she attended all the family functions on both sides, at her home and in her *sasural* – the naming ceremonies, *janiyas*, birthdays, engagements, weddings, visiting the hospitalised relatives and attending funerals in which the glamorous Juno stood out in the manicured crowd. At home she was graciousness personified, albeit more than a bit cuttingly.

"Ammi," she told her mother-in-law, "We have to maintain the standard set by Lata and Rita Didi, don't we? How will it look if I stop going to the Club and its various functions, just because they are not here now?" Cutting off the old woman's protests about expenses, she continued, "There is Dada's money and your son's as well. You know I never spend a penny on myself. My brothers abroad send me everything, from underwear to *saris* to purses and sandals, even cosmetics and pins. What do I spend anything on? Only on Sonu's school fees and my brothers send enough for that. After all, they are his Mamas."

But what of her own personal needs? Laajjo was young and good-looking. She had loved life in its full. Attending all the social events in the world could not compensate for having lost her husband so young? What was it that brought that glow to her face and eyes and that shift in the eyes of her mother-in-law?

Laajjo had taken a job. "Had I stayed back in the US, wouldn't I have worked there? So why not here?" She overrode Dadi's objections saying her mother-in-law did not mind. And she overrode Damayanti's by quoting Dadi.

The work was good and so was the money apparently, although her mother-in-law, Damayanti, was never able to figure out what her timings actually were. But she could not complain. Laajjo was smart enough to fit all social obligations with her office timings and managed to work overtime, which had her boss, the handsome Mr. Menon dropping her home so often that Damayanti got used to seeing him. The money flowed in, bringing in a phone and servants to make life easier, a company chauffer-driven car which allowed Damayanti to make a grand entry at the various functions and *pujas*, even offer a lift to Dadi!! That quite made the old lady's day and emboldened Laajjo to push the envelope even further.

"Ammi," she said one day, "I need to go to Bombay for some office work."

"What work?"

"It's a very big conference. I have to go to make notes and to keep all the information available for Mr. Menon. He'd be lost if I don't go and the company would lose a big contract worth crores."

"*Na, beta, na.* He has been so kind to you. One cannot always just take, one has to give also. You go and do your duty. I'll take care of Sonu."

Dadi had to choose that Sunday to visit. "Where's Laajjo?"

"Mummy has gone to Bombay on office work," said Sonu importantly.

Dadi looked at Sonu's grandmother. "Office work on a Sunday?"

The old lady had obviously not thought of that angle at all. She tried to explain but Dadi remained sceptical. "Where is she staying?"

"I did not ask. I'm sure the office would know," Dadi made a mental note to check it out with Parvati, who professed total ignorance.

After that, there was no holding back Laajjo. Her old assertiveness resurfaced. Only a few dared to query the details of her startling rise from being a clerk to an Assistant General Manager in a very short order, with a new house paid from a company loan, boarding school for Sonu and frequent outstation trips. After some time, Damayanti got so used to seeing Mr. Menon in the house that on occasion, she actually retired to her bedroom, while Laajjo and Mr. Menon sat nursing drinks and watching a late night movie on TV. "I don't like these English movies," she would protest.

Of course, it went beyond the late night movie. But if the old lady heard or saw, she kept it strictly to herself. Laajjo posed prettily as the ideal daughter-in-law in public, so who would believe otherwise? Only Dadi and Parvati. The latter would hear no evil, speak no evil and see no evil in her daughter and the former did not take up the issue when Damayanti refused to meet her eyes whenever the topic arose.

*****

8

BAGGAGE AUNTY

A dulcet voice rose above all the others in the *aarti*. Then followed it up with the *bhajans* praying for the departed soul. A quick look revealed the source of the dulcet voice, which came as a shock. That dulcet voice emanating from that mis-shapen body?

The *kathakar* introduced the singer as Radha and her companions crowding around as her mother Premila, Masi Satya and her ethereal cousin, Anita, as if to disguise the source of that sound.

It was a wonder that the delicate beauty of Premila had not found any replication at all in her daughter, the proverbial Beast of the Beauty, a gracious, talkative lady who had been the toast of her community in her day? The daughter was dark and ill-proportioned. Her only saving grace was her voice. Who would imagine that dulcet sound emanating from that body?

But all attention was focused not on the dulcet voice or its owner, but on her aunt Satya, the original Baggage Aunt, who had come home after staying abroad for decades.

Satya was busy with her own thoughts, ruminating over the events of the last few weeks, and as usual, drawing up the mental lists as she prepared for the future. For once in her life, she was the centre of the family attention and not her beautiful sister.

The families, parents, aunts, uncles, cousins on all sides of the family, even the respective in-laws used to hang on her every word.

They just couldn't get over the fact that their proverbially ugly duckling had blossomed into a rich, golden-egg laying duck. That she had taken that drunkard husband of hers in hand, carved out a profession for herself, raised her numerous children on that income and actually amassed enough to be able to afford a more-than-respectable dowry for her eldest daughter!

It was not as big as the one Premila was lying out, but it was enough to attract good proposals. Her daughter would lead a comfortable life, even if it meant Satya rearranging herself to start all over again, this time all by herself without Amma or Anita.

Of course, it was these qualities of her mother which had weighed in Anita's favour. No one in the family could get over the fact that their ugly duckling's offspring was an ethereal beauty.

On the other hand, the delicate beauty of Premila had not found replication at all in Radha, her daughter, the proverbial Beast in the Beauty, who was dark, plump, ill-proportioned, cursed with coarse hair at all the most unattractive places and to top it all, an ill temper. Her only saving grace was her voice. They shook their heads at the sounds that came out of Radha.

Such discussions had dominated their stay. Satya had been called upon umpteen times to recount with fresh detail and embroidery, the dramatic tale of how she came to be called the "Baggage Aunty" whose fame had spread far and wide, a precursor to the worldwide jet setting Baggage Aunties of the later decades.

*****

The Beginning

The clouds over the plunging deck, Satya recalled, had been as ominous as those of the Partition that they had put behind them.

Her mother, Kalawanti, one of Amma's daughters, died in the run up to the riots. Some remained, not blinkered, but helpless. How can one decide on leaving the century-old homes?

Her father, Hassanmal had not yet plunged into any post retirement trade. Therefore, he did not have the hassle of selling off a business, or transferring it for the duration of the trouble, as many optimists did. When Premila's husband wrote asking him to dispatch her immediately with the children to Singapore, he turned to Satya, "Your husband Bhaghu has not written yet, but since he's been there for so many years, he must be earning enough to support you, even if he doesn't send money home. Have faith in God. Go with your sister. I will pay for all your passages. Once you both are safe with your husbands, I will also leave."

In no time, Satya and her sister Premila were on board ship, heading for Singapore.

"Those two may be sisters. But, by Jove, what a difference! A new, silk *sari* every day, compared to those which have seen better days. One wears those lovely embroidered *saris*, trailing dust behind her and tripping over the pleats in front, showing off the pretty face and big eyes. "

"The Ugly One is at least neat and she obviously looks after Madame." Gossip followed their progress on the decks.

Premila had taken after her delicate mother, fair skin, long lashes, fringing doe eyes and the need for constant looking-after, not to trip over her *sari* when walking down the stairs.

"Was Ammi all that helpless?" Satya often wondered.

The plus point was that the constant vigil kept Satya too busy to brood over her title of the 'Ugly One'. "Was it my fault? That I have taken after my tall, gaunt and ugly grandfather?"

Height in a woman was not considered ladylike. "How can a man look after a woman who looks at him in the eye, or worse, look down at him?" her Dadi used to say of her long sallow face in which her huge eyes stood out when the long oiled hair were tightly plaited.

Satya had learnt to keep her face impassive. Otherwise, she would have spent her life weeping over her plain looks. Pitying glances were tolerable. The horrified ones... "Allah, am I that ugly? How did Dada get me married off then?"

*****

The early days in a new land with a strange Bhaghu were aggravated by the differences in the establishment of the two sisters.

Premila had the perfect setting for her ripe beauty, a sunny villa atop a hill, terraced gardens watered by an artificial stream falling off a series of miniature waterfalls to end in a lily pool.

Her Hill-top villa boasted of an impressive entrance into a serene interior dotted with masses of exotic flowers, huge verandahs, one large enough to hold what was called a 'Ping-Pong table' and generous balconies. High-roofed bedrooms were no problem to keep cool and scented; the efficient staff turned out delicious meals to tempt Madame's non-existent appetite, killed by her constant stream of complaints about the life in these 'foreign parts'.

For both the sisters, the round dining table was the piece *d' resistance* amongst the many wonders of the Big House. Dishes were laid out on a lazy Susan that rotated slowly to allow everyone to serve himself. Their eyes had shot up in wonder when they had first seen it.

Compared to all that cool scented elegance, Satya's home reflected her sad nickname. The house was located in one of the seedier localities. She recalled ruefully Premila's husband had tried to dissuade her from taking up residence there when they had landed.

Dark, sombre, only with two small skylights to provide occasional sunlight, the rooms were generous enough; but it had taken three whole days of dusting, scrubbing and washing to make it slightly habitable.

The staff, that existed under a drunken master, had fled at the advent of a Madame. Only an old maid, Amah had stayed on. Was it loyalty or the doubt of not finding another job at that advanced age? She lived to prove her weight in gold.

After the first visit, Satya took a long while to go again. There was no need to pretend. More than clearing the house, setting up the house on a shoe-string budget was a daunting task. With no apparent job, Bhaghu came home drunk every evening and got her pregnant straight off. She cursed her fertility, which produced a string of daughters. In this alien land, she dared not risk her life in the hands of a strange *Dai.* What would become of her daughters, with that drunken father?

Satya immersed herself in her home. Going up to the Hill house was an agony. It meant acknowledging the contrast between the two houses, seeing her sister, Premila blossoming out to full-blown rose proportions and complaining incessantly, and encountering those intense eyes of Premila's husband who took in Satya's every detail, nary an expression on his inscrutable face on the rare occasions when her timing failed her and he was home when she reached the Big House.

Often she mulled over the injustice done to her own little girls. She deprived them of the villa's numerous pleasures which they could not afford in their squalid little home. Sadly she consoled herself by thinking, "The less they go, the less they'll realise that most of their clothes and things are hand-me-downs".

For the taciturn man, the fleeting apparition of his sister-in-law, seen so rarely, was an unbearably painful ecstasy. In his eyes, the 'Ugly One' was the essence of the earth, a sturdily well-built woman, now exuding a raw, earthy sexiness, long raven hair, ripe breasts and a generous, fertile bottom, intense eyes wide open to the world without any silly rose tints and an indomitable courage.

In his eyes, the sight of Satya standing tall despite her sad lot instead of tripping prettily over her pleats made her Beauty came off worse, though he never said so aloud. In his quiet diplomatic fashion, he ensured enough simple deals with Bhaghu to keep the home fires burning, which included sending home provisions from some of the commissions.

When he bought *saris* for his wife, he made sure to put together a careful selection of pretty pastel prints and earthy tones to ensure that some of the rejected new *saris* would find their way to the sister's wardrobe. Who would dare to comment on his purchases?

One fateful night there was a great clanging late at night. Satya stood atop her stairs, watching the old woman muttering ominously as she pulled back the bolts to open the heavy door. The mistress's question marks confronted a fresh shame.

He held up a grimy burden, a blabbering drunk reeking of wine and vomit, obviously fished out a gutter. One look at the sleep-dishevelled hair, a look of tension across her face and 'he' wordlessly slung the drunk over his shoulder and marched upstairs. The old woman pointed the correct door that was shut resolutely in her face. "This is not a pretty sight," he said firmly.

Satya sent Amah off to bed and entered the kitchen to brew some coffee, her head bowed in shame. How, she agonised, was she going to face her kid sister, after this?

The Wordless Watcher followed her with his eyes, every movement was a poem of grace, when her hands lifted to her eyes and the shoulders began to shake, he moved forward swiftly.

But the penalty for offering the assistance was heavy. In an instant, all the barriers had crashed and the mutual passion, so long held in check, could no longer be denied or held back. Then and there, they clung, with her stoned husband lying comatose upstairs. Not a word was exchanged; their looks said it all. Afterwards, when both were exhausted and her head bent in flushed shame, he dressed and let himself out of the house.

That was the last that Satya was to see of him for a long, long while. For she cut herself off as much as she could without raising suspicions from her sister; unable to meet those loving eyes, furious over the constant stream of pregnancies.

"Not again, Satya, why didn't you stop him? Even animals have seasons. Doesn't he ever stop?" Premila exclaimed. Satya put a protective arm over her swelling womb, burning with shame. The guilt, of betraying the innocent trust of her sister, bored a '*nasur*' into her soul.

At a chance meeting at Diwali, he saw for perhaps the first time, the unmistakable sign of the new pregnancy. His eyes bored into her, forcing her to look up and face the query in his eyes. A deep flush gave her away, before the tiny nod and the guilty turning away from the wife at his side.

"You must do something for Bhaghu. If you don't then Satya will die, and what will become of the girls?" Premila admonished her husband.

"Of course, dear. Haven't I thought over this all this while?"

He queried his own wisdom in confiding in her and hedged, "It is difficult to get anyone to trust him; he manages to lapse on most of the deals I set up for him. Maybe we can work out something which may appeal to that drunkard's restless soul and crazy nature."

His placid wife failed to note the venomous passion in her husband's voice.

Surprise, surprise! Bhaghu was not drunk when he came home. He was on a high as he explained his new project, "Several local traders are backing me. I'll take their goods and retail them abroad. There is a terrific demand for all these things."

Characteristically her mind flew to pragmatic details, "Who'll pay the fare and board if the goods are not sold?"

Behind this lie her unspoken worry of her impending pregnancy.

"Don't be an old woman. I'll get good commission. Your generous Jija is getting my ticket. I'll stay with my cousin in Jakarta, so there will be no expenses."

The ticket was another sting; she had little time to recover before the goods began to arrive, always in Bhaghu's absence so that she could deal with them.

She received them, checked, counted them and stacked them, ready to pack. There was an exquisite lacey lingerie, ready-mades, beautiful handbags, elegant footwear, tinned and powdered milk, canned fruits, cheeses and chocolates and other stylish foods, make-up, costume jewellery, crystal ware and scores of trinkets and novelties such as key chains, ball pens, cameras and radios in toys, apples and lighters etc. In short, all the sophistication and the trivia that could make life tolerable for the expatriate families abroad.

It rent her soul to be packing away such beauties for sale when she longed for something to lighten her own dull life. But after an initial moment's pangs, she banished such notions behind her pragmatism and buckled to the job of packing with the aid of Amah and Anita, whilst the second girl supervised the younger ones. Caught up in the excitement of such beautiful things entering their home for the first time, no one remembered to cross their fingers. Disaster struck with less than a week from the D-day. Bhaghu reached home drunk and spent the night vomiting his guts out. By morning, there was a raging fever, which did not break for over twenty-four hours. In desperation, a doctor was called in.

"I'll give him an injection. It's cholera. No chances can be taken. He cannot travel." Panic settled slowly into determination.

For the first time, Satya went to meet him at his shop. A quick look around the store confirmed her nagging suspicions, the majority of Bhaghu's goods were because of the courtesy of her other Lord.

With a bowed head, she took a deep breath and braced to meet his eyes, "I will be going to Bhaghu's place." For once, emotion fleeted across the impassive face.

"Sit down," he commanded, "Don't worry, he can always go later or I'll send someone else." He glanced pointedly at her swollen belly. "After all, a woman..."

He did not know what he triggered.

"Yes, I am a woman. Bhaghu's unfortunate woman who tolerates his drinking, his womanising, his vomit, his seed, everything. If I can take that and fulfil all his contracts here, I can fulfil his contracts elsewhere too. Being a woman has not stopped me from beatings, why should it stop me from earning profits which will benefit my children?"

The raw passion in her voice stilled his tongue, stunning the onlookers. She took a deep shaking breath and declared

"It is final. Please see that the tickets are transferred to my name."

And then, in a softer tone, she said, "Don't worry, I'll retail better than a drunk and be back home before the confinement."

Little did Satya realise that this trip meant embarking on a life-long enterprise, sparked off by an unknown as yet and unlikely inspiration.

Her seventy-two hour journey oscillated between stomach-wrenching apprehensions and invigorating confidence, between excitement and fear and above all the wonder of being alone.

The exhilarating feeling of being free of all ties, no bemoaning husband, no complaining sister, no daughters to run after, feeling no guilt at his absence or presence... she was free to be herself, for once in her careworn lifetime.

"Why can't I be allowed one grace from God, of a love which would not make me so guilty?" she pondered. The guilt weighed her soul down as it meant betraying her sister, whom her father had entrusted to her care.

But Satya was too pragmatic a soul to dawdle for long. Mentally she squared her shoulders and ran over her lists the nth time.

*****

Satya's inspiration: Ruku Dadi.

Satya landed up, not at her cousin's place (another of Bhaghu's mistakes) but at a room in a community hall round the corner from the cousin's home, facing the railway track that cut through Jakarta.

It was a family of three, the spindly, bespectacled Manu whose mild manners were as apologetic as his wife Lekha's were assertive. Manu seemed to apologise for being alive at all. How he sold a thing as a salesman was a mystery for Satya.

Lekha wore the pants, actually escorting Manu to work so he would not lose himself at some congenial stopover half the day.

Lekha's relationship with her mother-in-law was ambivalent. They seemed fond of each other, bantering amicably as they ran the house with endless streams of visitors and precarious finances; but the younger woman made no secret of the fact that she blamed her mother-in-law for her weakling husband.

Widowed shortly after her arrival, Bhaghu's Aunt, Ruku Dadi had decided to raise her son in Jakarta, rather than risk uncertain welcome, maybe even curses reserved for a widow in India.

Her late husband's 'estate' consisted of a small plot with a handkerchief garden, of four coconuts trees, a couple of plantains craftily swamped inside the kitchen waste water, the obligatory tulsi fronting the house. There was no money in the bank, the only plus point was that he owed no money to anyone.

"The house was quite unsaleable, barely enough for a passage home. Home to what? To receive curses for 'finishing off' my husband? Living all my life as a burden? I decided I was better off here with no elder males to dictate to me. Looking back, I still feel that was the right decision. My son has turned out just like his father, or your husband, for that matter," Ruku Dadi confided in Satya, "At least I was lucky in getting him a smart educated wife."

The youthful widow then clawed her way to first her survival and then respectability. Which community will allow its widows to live in peace?

"I used to do sewing, embroidery, cooking for parties, anything for some money. The women here stood by me wonderfully, giving me as much work as possible, along with it fair money. How much did Manu and I need then? But the house was in terrible shape, I had to rebuild it. How did he live here before we came? He even had a local woman and these locals build well..." With a shock, Satya realised that she was talking impassively about a mistress, as if that did not matter.

Ruku Dadi added a proper kitchen and bathroom to the verandah off the tiny bedroom. The hall was already dominated by a collection of prayer books, its walls choc-a-bloc with icons and pictures of every God, Goddess and saint ever depicted on paper. Satya was wonderstruck at the sight; she marvelled over where Bhaghu had expected to stay here with all his trunks.

Dadi dispassionately said, "All of us learn to survive, despite our men, dead or alive. I should have died, when the first drunk entered my house after my husband's death, in the dead of night. There was no lock. Those came later, after my repairs. In this seedy area along the railway tracks, who will listen or follow a woman's outraged cry?

But I did not die. How could I go onto those tracks, so near and so far, leaving behind a defenceless baby in an alien land? I lived on, with a butcher's knife under my pillow and tin buckets on both sides of my door and windows at night to give me warning.

It took three swipes, just three big ones. The first one was bang on someone's nose. The second on another one's thigh and the third fellow died, when he staggered onto the railway track with deep cuts across his face and walked into a passing train.

"After that," she went on in a totally neutral voice, "no one troubled me. But for years, no man here would meet my eyes. Three doors were closed to me for ever."

Lekha piped up, "That was entirely their loss. Their women continued to support Dadi."

"Do you also call her Dadi?

"Of course. She is *Jagat Dadi*. In the beginning, their support was covert. They would send work with their servants, not letting their husbands know, because of the scandal and all. But the men found themselves daunted by a very potent challenge."

The older woman strove to keep her *bahu's* excitement in check. "I had read all the books with my father and could quote extensively from the *Ramayana*, the *Mahabharata*, *Gita*, *Upanishads*, *Guru Granth Sahib*, Vivekananda and others. That acted as a balm for the wounded souls of the women. It eased their homesickness and sorted out many problems at home. Gradually I was invited for their *satsangs* and *kirtans*, followed by the birthdays and the naming ceremonies. Over the years, my little temple became the strength of the community. Later, when the house became too small to accommodate the crowds at festivals, they built the community hall round the corner."

Satya looked carefully at the tiny, white-clad woman with large capable hands, struck afresh by her serene expression and the calm eyes which embraced all the sorrows that made a beeline to her door, making her the fulcrum of the community which had, once upon a time, tried to edge her into another role altogether. Her eyes, she noted, were never lowered.

"Don't look down," Ruku Dadi admonished, "Rather look at the world straight in the eye, otherwise it'll not allow you to live. *Sharm-Haya* is not only a woman's *ghehena*, it can also become a death noose. Don't allow it to become that."

"Yes," seconded Lekha, "Look carefully and digest her. These are the shoulders which bear the sorrows of our little world. All the joys and sorrows of men and women make a beeline at our door, to this High Priestess, for lessons of love and advice. Can you understand why I cannot hate her even though she had blighted my life with her son? My parents thought the world of her. They did not check on him. She did not enlighten them. Fate, she told me." In the hushed silence that followed the sudden darkness, Satya struggled to absorb the essence of the parable for her own troubled life.

Mulling over the story, Satya set to work, setting out her wares for easy retrieval on demand and carefully selecting suitable gifts for her hostesses.

"The demand is high," said Lekha. They estimated a week to sell off most of it. But Satya's sales pitch made everything vanish in just three days flat. Her book was full of orders with specific requests for items, colours etc.

"Come again soon," was a repeated plea, ignoring her obvious condition and fatigue. Satya rushed back, just in time, before her waters broke.

"*Aye hai*," wailed an apprehensive Amah, setting Anita to boiling water and sending Bhaghu off to fetch a midwife. "It is beyond me this time. Make yourself useful for a change," she ordered her boss with asperity.

Unlike her earlier confinements, this was not an easy birth. No one had time to wonder why, except that it was a double first, which included the first painful birthing and a first boy for Satya.

Bhaghu, Premila and the girls were delirious. Satya sought the old woman's eyes apprehensively. Despite reassurance, she examined her baby carefully before embracing him with a heartfelt sigh.

The baby's natural father only appeared on the *Chhat* (6th day), for the naming, his impassive face inscrutable as ever. Satya pointedly ignored the question in his eyes.

"She is refusing to come and rest at our house," said Premila prettily.

"Nonsense, I have to start coping with the next trip's stores. One more mouth to feed now," Satya retorted tartly. Confusion infused an unusual asperity in her voice, which did not go unmarked.

"These are not the things for which I got orders for. These won't sell."

"Stop your black tongue. Just because the sympathy of the people whom you sold your goods once, you think you know better than me. Just because these things have not come from your precious Jija's store."

"At least take the things I got the orders for."

"Just shut up and let me do my work."

Satya supervised the packing of Bhaghu's new goods and saw him off with severe foreboding. The wait for his return stretched from the planned seven to twenty-eight long days.

When he did come back, Bhaghu had more luggage than before, proceeding immediately on a roaring binge. After three days of listening to the bombast from his room, Satya broke her vows and approached him, on a Sunday at home.

"How long can I keep telling all the traders and others that he is sleeping? I've checked the stores and practically everything has come back, very little has gone at all. I had warned him. Secondly, he has brought stuff from there but no money," she sounded at the end of her tether.

When he came downstairs after his talk with Bhaghu, Satya barred his path. "Tell me."

"I'll look after it."

"Tell me first," the tone was level enough, but there was steel in the voice.

"Nothing sold in twenty-eight days, so he dumped some of it at the two shops and brought their stuff in exchange, barely covering passage and board. We'll have to return all the other goods."

An ominous silence descended on the house. Even the baby voice could barely be heard.

Two days later, Satya was at the shop. "I'll go, after weaning Sonu onto the powdered milk."

"No need of it. I'll send somebody or better still, lend you some money until Bhaghu..."

"Listen to me, I'll work for my children but I'll not beg for them." Once again, there was steel in her voice and it whip lashed across his large impassive face.

"Is that your final decision?"

"Yes. But I need your help to keep up the tempo. Bhaghu's recovering only to get drunk again..."

The welcome this time was distinctly subdued, unlike the earlier spontaneous one. Lekha spelt out the ugly truths.

"Bhaghu had not brought any of the things they ordered. He was drunk and tried to display *saris* draping them over a local practically nude in his bed. It was indecent," she shuddered.

Satya imagined that she saw suspicion or pity in everyone she encountered. Tensely, she searched each pair of eyes apprehensively until Ruku Dadi rebuked her.

"Satya, you have come to sell your goods, not to act as a detective to check up on Bhaghu. Disassociate yourself from his shadow. Don't even try to find out," she advised sagely. "It will only affect your behaviour with your clients. Meet people with your mind in a clean slate, as Satya, not as Bhaghu's wife. Why did you not fulfil those orders you had got?"

Satya looked at Dadi in the eyes, begging for unspoken understanding, before replying in a low voice, "I have brought them with me this time."

"Then deliver them properly." Before she left, Ruku Dadi read her another lecture, "Satya, don't just live, think also. Use your head. Everyone bears burdens. You have yours, that too, heavy ones. Don't add Bhaghu's to yours, instead make him part of your burden, if you must."

Satya gave her a startled look.

"What does that mean?"

"Do you want to be forever picking up the pieces he has broken? Why not work yourself instead? You would make more money, instead of more enemies. Drunkards never succeed in anything but losing money and making enemies. Is that what your children need? Find a way out for yourself."

Satya mulled over this question all the way home where a fresh crisis awaited her, in the form of a rejuvenated Bhaghu rearing to go once again, backed by his loutish drinking friends. "Who will finance this trip?"

"Haven't you brought the money with you?"

"That is to pay for the last time's losses, provisions and the school fees next month and..."

"Keep your bloody money to yourself. You think you have bought the Mint with a few hundred. I have people to back me..." he strutted, reeling out names.

Appalled at what she saw, Satya realised that these were the vultures who led men like Bhaghu to losses and then bankruptcy. She agonised for a whole day and night. Only one thought came to her mind that, "Bhaghu must be stopped."

She was reluctant to go up the Hill again; that inevitable tussle of wills and the shaming guilt that suffused her soul whenever she met her sister and her husband together. Somehow, at the shop, it was different. That was business. Even then, she kept her visits to the barest minimum.

Amah gave her a vigorous massage and gentle words of wisdom, "Cool your brain, then only will the answer come to you."

"Tell me, Amah; how can we stop him from going again? He'll only ruin everything. We'll lose even this house," she moaned out her greatest fear, which included the roof over her children's heads, the last vestige of her own standing, without taking total charity of her younger sister.

The old woman gave her a considering look. "You want to stop him from going. Then how will we eat after two months?"

"Then I'll go again, but..."

"But what?"

"Not if he's gone in between. He will ruin the entire market for me." It was such a relief to unburden her greatest fears as she retold the sordid story.

"So, Bhaghu sir must not go and if the children are to be brought up without begging," Satya gave the old woman a startled look which she met her face on and continued, "you have to go, not once or twice, but again, and again. Do you have the strength? Do you want to? Can you do it?"

"Where is the question of can or want? I have to, where is the choice? What to do about Bhaghu?" Amah led her on the new uncharted path with shrewd questions.

"What is Bhaghu's main problem?"

"Drinking. That is why he cannot work."

"So let him drink and keep himself out of mischief, but you go for work."

Satya looked at the old woman sharply. Amah met her eyes with an audaciously mischievous glint, "Yes, I said that, let him drink, you work. Let him have his drink in his own room upstairs. Morning and evening, let a bottle be available to him. He will have no time for those vultures, no energy to go out. You work. I will look after the children."

The younger woman looked at her in awe, absorbing all that she said.

"You have to break some eggs to make an omelette. Break yours and for God's sake, stop getting pregnant."

Slowly Amah allowed the import to sink in. It lifted the pressure off Satya's heart and the heavy cloud from her head. Mentally and physically squaring her shoulders, Satya let out a long quivering breath. What had to be done, should be done.

"Let's get on with it then."

"Not so fast, my lady. Everything should happen at the proper time. First, we shall sleep on this and then act slowly. Let it be a natural development," with gentle but firm strokes, Amah pushed her towards sleep.

At the shop, he watched Satya's determined entry. There was something ominous about her stance.

"What have you decided?" he asked abruptly

"I need your help to keep up this tempo. Plus some financial aid and..."

"That is not what I meant."

"You," said Satya very deliberately, "are my sister's husband and I am Bhaghu's wife. Let us always remember that." The shake in her voice got through. The man bowed his head.

Quietly, he put out his hand for the lists in her hand. Very methodically she shuffled through them. "These are from here. The other stuff I'll get elsewhere. Just tell me where to get the cheapest."

After a few stiff moments, they settled down to the task. She read out her requirements and he called out the names of the wholesalers and the shops, whom to contact and phone numbers which she listed neatly in her diary.

Satya's lists had come to stay for decades to come.

*****

The Ending

Her sister's incessant chatter brought her back to the present. "How will he react to the two proposals, which we have finalised? What do you think? You have got the pick of the boys. No doubt, my Radha will go into a rich family, but I really like your Shankar... so cultured and well mannered and such jolly parents too. Anita is a lucky girl..."

Satya hardly heard the rest; it was the first statement which had seared itself in her mind how will he react, will he approve?

She wondered whether he would come to the quay to receive them, and actually come face to face with her, after all these years of carefully avoiding each other, of working through the intermediaries who did not matter and did not know anything of the past.

As the ship drew close, four pairs of eyes scanned the quay. The two pairs were the young ones, dancing with a shy delight and beating hearts in anticipation of the ribbing in store. Of the two pairs of the older ones, one grew more and more anxious as the group on the quay defined itself.

There was the dearly beloved figure, that massive thickset frame topped by a well-remembered salt-and-peppered leonine head and a thick beard which disguised the square-cut jaw.

Premila let out a gurgle of laughter, "Look, just look, he's grown a beard. After all these years! Once upon a time, you know, I had nagged and nagged him to grow one. It was so fashionable then, looked so elegant. But he didn't listen to me then. See now, he missed me so much that he must have remembered that this was one wish he had not fulfilled, so he did it in my absence. He's giving me the beard as a coming home present..."

The effect of the beard was totally different on her sister. Wild eyes scanned the rest of the group at the quay. That scalawag Bhaghu with his usual drunken grin, why had he come at all? The gaggle of youngsters, the girls, and was that Suresh?

It seemed as if overnight he had been pulled up by the ears to beanstalk proportions. He stood tall, almost touching his uncle's shoulders. But that face! That face and the shape of the head, the square cut of the jaw, the resemblance...

Satya turned frenzied pleading eyes towards her sister, clutching her hands dumbly begging forgiveness and understanding... but Premila was oblivious, still prattling on about the beard.

Satya knew at once why the beard had been grown – not to please Premila – but to disguise the tell-tale cut of the jaw – even now he was protecting her and their precious secret.

As she turned anguished eyes to her younger sister, the blood rushed to her head, pounding at her temples. A terrible pain shot through her and she clutched her chest, staggering back with one thought in her mind, "She must not know, she must not know..."

None of the excited, twittering trio noticed Satya's staggering back. No one saw her lose her balance to tumble down the hatchway, gone for ever, carrying her guilty secret with her.

*****

9

NEELIMA'S DAUGHTERS

Almost two decades down the line, Neelima's daughter, Nikita looked out at the ocean with unseeing eyes. Neither the cormorants, nor the waves, nor the gentle giants of the azure sea pleasured her senses anymore.

The troubled eyes saw in the waves the image of her daughter Rashmi, the teary eyes opened wide in terror at the thought of losing her mother.

"Ma, you can't leave me."

"No, darling, I'll not leave you here. I'll see you safely to your *sasural* first."

"Then they'll slaughter me there, when you go off."

Nikita looked into her daughter's dark brown eyes with a sigh. She seemed to remember putting her own mother through a similar dilemma, demanding silence, for the sake of peace in a daughter's household half way across the world.

It had not worked then. Ultimately truth would be out. For all her ultra-modern upbringing in the Caribbean, her bobbed hair, jeans, mini skirts and her made-up face, Rashmi remained at heart a conventional Indian; she was, if anything, more home bound than even her India-born cousins, who had been exposed to the more progressive trends when they went to college there, while Rashmi had lived life out in what was little better than an Indian ghetto, more mental than physical, on an island with a romantic name, Aruba.

Her parents and grandparents had come here long ago, bringing with them the India that they had left behind. That mental India never went forward the way, the actual India did.

"Rashmi," Nikita rasped, "If you want a traditional marriage, I'll give you one. If you have any one, any one at all in mind, tell me and let me work on it. But for God's sake, don't expect to hold me up to ransom for the rest of my life – just to keep the peace in your still prospective home. Ye Gods! How did I manage to produce such a spiritless specimen?"

Rashmi was Asperity personified. "If I remember correctly, you married at Dadi's bidding. And continued to keep the peace in the house only because of her and grandpa's temper. As long as that old Dour Face was alive, there was no talk of your loving or even liking anyone else. No sooner he's dead."

"Shut that pretty mealy mouth of yours. Have you any idea what you're talking about?"

"Yes. For one, what do you think will happen to Papa?"

That struck a raw nerve. Nikita knew that any move would shatter the equanimity of her pot bellied, laid back husband, precisely because he could never imagine that any such thing could happen, that any woman would have the courage to break away from marriage.

At times, Nikita wondered how her husband was, in some matters, so much like her father, Hari, that gentle giant who used to quail before his own father and could never take a decision, personal or commercial, without prolonged agonising and would then put his foot into his mouth in full measure.

All her life, Nikita had seen her mother, Neelima take all decisions, taking hold to keep the business, her husband and the family together. Nikita recalled her last meeting with her mother, when they had discussed her painful dilemma, her love for a man other than her wedded husband and Rashmi's mutiny.

Nikita had examined her mother's face carefully, delving deep into her eyes. There was a medley of emotions, sorrow at the turn of events, sympathy reaching out to her daughter's obvious pain and behind it, a touch of the 'I told you so' malice at the granddaughter's mutiny, plus 'Now you know what I have gone through'.

Neelima herself had lived through a painful childhood and equally painful marriage – her mother, Bhagwanti was always bitter over Yvette, her father's second wife, a French lady. After making her acquaintance with her long absent father and his new wife, Neelima was always torn between her loyalties to her two mothers, two women who stood at the opposite ends of the social spectrum.

Bhagwanti, in a white sari, oiled *chuttiya*, and unable to overcome the burden that life had placed on her shoulders as a deserted woman...

"Ma, why do you wear white all the time?"

"It is so much easier. No questioning of repeating a *sari* if you wear white all the time. Don't have to waste time contemplating what to wear every time I have to go out, like your chachi does all the time. What is the fashion, what colour is out? What fabric is in? And besides who is there to get ensnared with all that? Why waste so much time on looks when there is no one to look?"

Her stepmother, Yvette, was so elegant, loving and cheerfully full of life, despite that 'Second Woman' label inflicted on her by an adamant family. How willingly had she stepped into Neelima's life, to transform her as a teenager, stepped into the shadows during her marriage to give Bhagwanti her due as the mother and then much later, when Neelima's life was threatening to fall apart, to offer moral and financial support to enable Neelima and Hari to build a life of their own, away from the shadow of his father's business empire.

Neelima's marriage could have been almost as disastrous as her mother's. Her husband, Hari was so much the opposite of her go-getting father. If Neelima had not taken charge of her and his life, she might have found herself in as much of a plight as her mother.

Hari could not say 'hoo' to a cat. His father used to beat him up in front of his newly wed bride. Although Neelima and Hari had spent a lifetime away from India in the Canary Islands, Hari's father's shadow remained over their lives, across the seven seas.

Nikita's husband was selected for her by Dadi and he was in the same mould as Hari. Initially after her life shifted from the Canary Islands to the Caribbean ones, Nikita had tried her best to rally Ram.

"Why don't you do something of your own? I'll help you."

But he was too complacent, actually too lazy to take up that responsibility. Better to take home a monthly pay packet and let the boss worry about the profits and the losses.

Neelima and Nikita sat looking long and hard into each other's sorrowful eyes. At last, the older woman spoke, "I can understand your grief; haven't I lived through it? Now your daughter wants to tie you down to this world, this society of ours, just so that she can have a comfortable time in her *sasural*, which has not yet been found for her. She is looking for the security which she never got from her father. And she does not want to jeopardise her chance of finding it, in case your going away is held against her."

At last the daughter reacted, startled by the accusation. Neelima continued, "Yes, I know. I have known this for some time now. Why do you think your father's hair went grey overnight? Never mind, now nothing can be done. Nothing could be done years ago when your grandfather, my father found someone else and stayed away. And nothing can be done now.

"You are condemned, like me to the heartache of loss, for you, it means the loss of a daughter you loved. Just as I watched my mother forever sorrowing over my father and not realising what had happened in his life; similarly you will be torn in two parts and broken by the effort of keeping up appearances, despite the heartaches and the odds.

"And, my love, I can offer you nothing, except a shoulder to weep on whenever you need it."

Nikita broke down on her mother's shoulder. "What do I do with Rashmi? She's rejecting all the boys right, left and centre. Could it be just to delay, knowing that I want to go away?" she queried in a weepy voice.

"Rashmi is your daughter and she has never learnt to be anything but selfish. Let her stew in her own foul juices for a while. You wanted only one child and you made sure that you got only one. But see the repercussions. She thinks only of herself. It is not as if she is too young to understand what a travesty your marriage has been."

Having seen the burden on her mother's shoulders because she always took charge, after gauging Ram, Nikita took pains to always prod him forward, instead of taking the lead herself. She devoted herself frenetically to her only child, Rashmi. Despite tremendous pressure from her in-laws for a boy, she refused to try for a second child.

"Ram will not be able to afford another daughter," she declared firmly. Those were the days before amniocentesis and selective abortions. For years, they had muddled along, until Dayal Bhatia came into her life. He was everything that Ram was not – dynamic, go-getting, cheerful and talkative – yet with a sense of values which made Nikita recall her early run-in with Ram's lack of them, early in her marriage. Would Dayal have done that?

Nikita recalled the run-up to her marriage, all her efforts at warding off a union with a person who projected nothing by insipidness, and the leering, laughing responses from her cousins and aunts, "Why are you worried? There is nothing to worry about. Hasn't your sister Saloni gone through an arranged marriage too? And she's doing well for herself, with her husband in Panama, sending her all the money she needs and more... All she had to do is go through with a jazzy wedding and all he had to do is fuck her. Actually, he only does that once in a while. You know the guys only come home in about two to three years. In between, she also gets to flirt with all the others brothers-in-law and the rest who drop in periodically. And for the rest of life, we'll be there. Haven't all of us also led our lives like that? In your case, he'll not take you initially to the US. But since you've never lived in India, it will be a nice change for you, won't it?"

Nikita knew about her sister Saloni. Hers had been a convenient marriage dictated by the elders, just as so many others which were the order of the day. Her life was a placid conventional one, no high passions, no dramatic, gut wrenching lows, just a whirl of social, woman-centric events, engagements, weddings, funerals, *janiyas*, birthdays, *pujas*, *satsangs*, anything that gave a little high in the absence of the husbands who were thousands of miles away.

Petty issues dominated her life.

'The gifts given to me during so-and-so's engagements were not good enough.' 'My sister-in-law only rings me once a month, although I call her every week.' 'So-and-so didn't say bye to me before leaving for her last trip abroad.' 'How could she forget me?' But life carried on, nevertheless, and quite smoothly, with occasional trips abroad, to Panama and to the US to visit her husband, to her *maika* in the Canary Islands and even a Paris trip to her maternal grandfather and one to Hong Kong for a sister-in-law's wedding splash there.

But it had not worked out quite that way for Nikita. And recriminations had rent the air during her visits home, very early in the marriage.

"See the mess you've landed me into. You created it, now you sort it out."

"Nikita, you can't talk like that. It is your marriage; you have to cope with it." Dadi was very firm. An assortment of cousins looked on, looking out for the outcome with keen interest. After all, what was at stake here could affect each one of them, now or in the near future.

"Not at all. Why should I cope alone? You were the one who made this marriage; you have to cope with it."

"What do you mean by that, girl?"

"You found Ram, approved of him and got me married to him. I'd said it then, and I'm saying it now, I married Ram because you said so. Now you cope with him, I can't."

"Don't be silly. Even if we found the boy, you have married him..."

"On your instructions."

"Why did you? You should have found someone of your own."

"But you refused to even countenance that."

"Don't you remember why?"

"He did not belong to our so called precious caste. What is that caste doing about this now? All of you were so adamant, threatened to commit suicide, refused to eat, and threatened never to see me again or talk to me and all that drama. So I told all of you to go ahead and find a boy you wanted. Shouldn't you have been more responsible in checking his background?"

"How?"

"All you checked was his caste qualifications. What else? A good job? But for how long? I have been married for six years and he has changed five jobs. All he does is pick fights with the boss, take debts and then drinks off his shame. Now..."

Neelima, Nikita's mother spoke up, "Now what? Why are you doing this, Nikita, why blame us? You married him, didn't you? What if you had married a guy you picked and he had made a wrong move? Even love marriages break down."

"That would have been my decision and I would have dealt with it. This decision was taken by you people; you must accept the responsibility and deal with it."

"Deal with what? A husband's drinking habit? Every second man has it and every tenth woman abroad drinks too. So what is the big deal? Such a disaster?"

"I am not talking about drinking, ma. Please understand that. I can survive. I know there are the chachas and the mamas to fall back on. But I will not prostitute myself for anyone, not even with my wonderful caste husband." Raw passions erupted painfully in her voice. "I'll not talk of committing suicide or any of that shit. I have a life and I want to live it happily, not for the happiness of my caste or the husband that the caste has provided."

Mother and daughter locked gazes at each other, shock and unspoken grief chasing through the older woman's heart and accusation and tension in the younger pair.

In both pairs of eyes, there was a mute plea for understanding.

Nikita shook herself back into the present. "Ma, how can I ignore my own child?"

"In this matter, aren't you ignoring your own husband?"

"How much will it matter to him? He has plenty of sisters' and bhabhis' shoulders to cry on about a vagrant wife. They'll get him married again in no time. This time, he'll make sure he gets someone who is not constantly pushing him. After all these years of struggling with his dead weight, he matters less to me than Rashmi. She is the daughter I've devoted a lifetime on."

"Well, as I see it, you have not done a very good job of it. She knows the score at home. And is all set to marry herself. She is the one who sees all the English movies and reads all those novels. Why is she making such a song and dance about you? Are you the first married woman in the world to fall in love? Or the first in our community?"

The attraction between Nikita and Dayal had been there from day one. He and his wife had come for the wedding of their daughter's sister-in-law. Nikita and Ram were representing Ram's father who was the groom's uncle. All through the various events, Nikita was so conscious of Dayal that she went out of her way to avoid the light-hearted flirting which was so much a part of any wedding scene. It was difficult to keep control and not let her eyes give her away.

Dayal was based in Colombo. He had a married daughter in Canada and a handsome son who too was there at the wedding. When someone casually mentioned that he would make a good match with Rashmi, Ram put his foot down, "They are Bhatias. Sindhis but not Bhaibunds. I will not give my daughter there. Am I Rashmi's enemy? Anyways, she's still too young for marriage yet."

Rashmi was not even consulted and Nikita did not know whether to be relieved at not having Dayal as her daughter's father-in-law or furious with Ram for not even asking Rashmi before saying no.

It was several months later that news came through. "Remember Dayal Bhatia? The handsome father with a handsome son? His wife died."

"What? How did that happen?"

"It seems that she had a bad spell while they were visiting their daughter in Canada. When she was taken for a check-up, the doctors said it was pancreatic cancer, and that too in an advanced stage. They gave her three weeks, but she was gone before that."

"So quickly? How? She seemed hale and hearty when she was here?"

"Not quite. You met her for the first time. I felt she was looking pulled down but I thought maybe because her daughter was having trouble with her in-laws and all that. But who would have dreamt of this?"

Dayal, a widower? Nikita tried to keep a tight rein on herself, constantly looking at Ram and Rashmi. But in the next four years, whenever Nikita traveled, whether to the US or to India, she found herself bumping into Dayal socially everywhere. It hardly seemed like not being a Bhaibund had made any difference to Dayal's social acceptance. And that fatal attraction…

It did not escape the sharply tuned antenna of Neelima either. But she held her peace, waiting for Nikita to speak, knowing fully well that her daughter must be suppressing her feelings, not knowing whether Dayal shared them; would he take such a step? Would she? Divorce? What of her husband? Her beloved daughter? The family at large?

What will people say?

These were big questions, very big ones. On one momentous occasion, when Rashmi was out with her cousins, Dayal and Nikita managed to share a quiet lunch in the suburban anonymity of Bombay, holding hands on the table and looking into each other's eyes, for all the world like a love-struck teenagers, recalled Nikita with a wry smile.

The problems were too many, too big. Dayal's daughter was married, but her in-laws were sticky people. Nikita had yet to get her daughter married. Would people accept a daughter-in-law from a divorced home? That was the problem number one.

Two, what would people say?

Three, even if they get over that, how can Nikita marry Dayal? What grounds did she have for a divorce? At this age?

It was all so hopeless. There seemed no way out. Agonised eyes met, hopelessness wrung in the hands which clinged into each other. Why didn't we ever meet when we were young and unattached? Now living halfway across the world? There was little chance of a divorce. Ram would never accept 'mutual consent' and there were no other definitive grounds.

Perhaps they could just go away and live together. After all, hadn't the Sindhi guys been doing that for centuries, living with foreign women in foreign parts, while their wives lived in India with the family? Shyam and Maya, Bhagwanti and Dada? Dayal was not a foreigner, he was an Indian, Sindhi and a widower. But Nikita was very much a married woman, and a Sindhi to boot. To live without getting a divorce from Ram and without getting married to Dayal? The thought itself was so frightening.

It took months of agonising across oceans for Nikita to learn to live with herself. But how did Rashmi stumble on her secret? And Neelima? She never knew how she gave herself away to the two persons in the world dearest to her. Whose happiness mattered to her? Was there no way out?

Nikita had a run-in with Ram. Had Rashmi told him? How much? He was voluble and vicious. Finally Nikita answered back, "Only your ego is preventing you from accepting the fact that our marriage was hardly a marriage. So don't work so hard at making it worse. Perhaps life will give you the opportunity to regret the terrible things you have done to wreck sorrow on those around you, merely to please your ego. Things change, but unfortunately, not male thinking. Bad luck!" After that, they barely communicated.

Rashmi was on the verge of mutiny when they arrived in India. Fortunately, her grandma, Neelima was there too. She sized up the situation wisely.

"Rashmi, do you remember Nina Masi?"

"Ma's twin? I thought she was d..." her voice trailed away uncertainly. No one had spoken of Nina Masi ever since she could recall.

"Ma," burst out Nikita, "Where is Nina? It's been ages since I saw her. How is she? Is she in India? Have you met her?"

"She is very much here. Your papa has his own hang-ups. But how can I allow a daughter of mine to just drop out of sight? Now even he has accepted the situation."

"What situation?" piped in Rashmi, "What did Nina Masi do?"

"She fell in love and married him. And that is frowned upon in our..."

"Tell me the whole story."

"Let her tell you herself. We'll all go and see her," said Neelima firmly. "Nina and her husband are raising strawberries at a farm near Mahableshwar. It's a lovely place."

In a very quick order, they were racing off the highway. It wasn't a long drive, about three to four hours only, with constant changes of scene, from rolling plains dotted with factory sheds and fields to twisting around hills with scenic views thrown in, deep valleys dotted with patchwork fields.

They had chosen to surprise Nina. Both the husband and wife were out when they reached the farm. Nikita looked around with obvious pleasure at the well-preserved British-style bungalow with wide verandahs all around set in the middle of the estate. The blue china pottery and the delicate gold painting brought a host of childhood memories, of overcrowded drawing rooms of elderly aunts and uncles, of a Pekinese poodle with maliciously glinting eyes peeping out of the profuse hair, of wonderful jars filled with dozens of blooms, of gorgeous baskets of flowers in different shapes and flavours from mama's florist friends. Every Christmas was a different theme, childhood photos, different types of cakes, sweets and chocolates.

Christmas was the fairy visit time, of flowers and singing carols and delicious multi-layered cakes that took hours to make and seconds to melt in the mouth, and strange yet familiar dishes at the luncheon table with second helpings generously foisted to fill the bulging little bellies, replete with overeating, over feasting, over flowering, over caking and over listening.

The weather was lovely. It was not entirely the end of winter, not yet even spring proper. It was still cold enough to relish the warmth of a shawl spread over the shoulders. The warm sun splashing the garden was inviting. And it was a treat to watch the sunrays streaming into the bedrooms and on the beds. So inviting for a nap, with just a light *razai* thrown over one, to snooze off into, listening to some music, until Nina and Jagat made their appearance.

By that time, Rashmi had wormed out some of the story and the young woman was rearing to get at her aunt.

"How could she just go off like that and marry whom she wanted, without considering the effect on the family's status? And a non-Sindhi married man at that! People shouldn't be allowed to do such things, you know..."

Neelima gave her a stern look. "Don't you say silly things like that? Who are you to judge anyone? Who is anyone to judge another? Every person has their own compulsions and needs?"

Nikita and Nina were ecstatic at meeting each other after so long. Jagat looked on with some rancour and said, "So you finally remembered your twin? Did you never miss her, like she constantly did? What took you so long?"

Nikita was properly remorseful but Rashmi stepped in with her outbursts.

"How could you? Are all you sisters alike? Or is Saloni aunty the only sane one? Did you inspire ma? She also wants to marry at this age, when her first priority should be to get me married."

Nina was thoughtful as she looked straight into her niece's eyes and declared, "What can I say? Years ago, I did what I did, with greater constraints than intractable children and family. A wise old man advised me, "Look dear, it is only a question of a piece of paper. A piece of paper stands between your and your happiness. So first of all, decide, do you really feel that you want to grow old with him? And no other? Decide that first. Then we'll go to the next step.

"Now see, you know how much you love him and want him. His wife also knows how much he loves you and wants you. They haven't been near each other for two years now, but she'll not admit that and nor will she grant a divorce. Why should she? It is a question of her prestige, her status, her pride and her ego.

"So it may take all of seven to ten years to get that piece of paper which will say that the Government of India hereby declares that so and so are no longer man and wife.

"That piece of paper, or rather, its absence is going to keep you apart more effectively than the opposition of your parents. For the next ten years! By that time, you'll be thirty and he'll be forty. The so-called prime of life, but way past your youth. This means you would have lost a whole decade of your life, your dreams, possibly your chance to have healthy children of your own.

"For what? For that piece of paper? You'll never be able to recreate the joys of your youth ten years on. Those will be gone forever, slipping like sand through your fingers, into the Past. For what?

"Ten years on, your parents' objections will remain the same. Then they will ask why you are marrying a divorcee. They will be as adamant then, as they are today in asking why you want a married man.

"But, if by then you are already living together as man and wife and they see that you have made a go of it and succeeded in bringing up your family properly, they may begin to mellow.

"You have to decide whether you need that piece of paper to really love your Love. It is up to you."

"And what did you do?"

"I chose to love my Love and let that piece of paper go to the Hell. When it comes, it comes. And if it does not, let it be. I just left home. When I look back and see myself, I thank God that I was too young and too naïve to see the pitfalls I was skirting. So many things could have gone wrong, but did not. They say God is hard on lovers. I think He really looks out for us. So many things could have gone wrong.

"The day I left home, if my father had sent someone with me that would have been it. All my plans would have been sabotaged.

"Then I could have been discovered in the hotel where I was hiding but I wasn't.

"The day we had to give up the hotel room, Jagat had arranged for me to spend a few hours until my flight was scheduled to leave, in another room occupied by a friend, who was a bit of a notorious character. Jagat was late and I moved out of my room and just walked upto this guy's room and announced, 'Look, I'm...' This so-called notorious person just picked up his briefcase and left saying, 'I have an appointment. Make yourself comfortable.'

"Just imagine, a man with his reputation (which I was not aware of at that time), who knew that I had run away from home. He could have taken advantage of the situation but he didn't.

"When I reached my sister-in-law's place, she could have refused to take me in. After all, she had arranged Jagat's first marriage herself. But she took me in and looked after me until he arrived.

"After we got married and Jagat had to go away, anyone could have taken advantage of me, a naïve twenty one-year-old in a strange city, surrounded by strangers and no contact with home. I had burnt my boats. Anyone, the neighbours, his lusty cousins, the landlord, but no one did. Instead they all looked after me. Even Jagat could have abandoned me, rather than risk his reputation and the career loss. But he did not.

"He came back for me and we've survived. I'll not say happily ever after. It's been an adventurous lifetime, plunging from one crisis to another, but we've survived it all, grown old together, and bred a family. Thanks to that wise old man.

"Que, sera, sera, what will be, will be. And don't you try this guilt trip business all the time. Ma had accepted my decision to marry my heart." Nikita was startled.

"You know nothing of that. No one does, only ma and me. One day, ma and I went together. We walked and walked for so long and finally sat down on a bench near Sarasbaug. And I poured my heart out to her, everything, just everything. That Jagat would have to give up his government job and that we would have to migrate right away, to avoid embarrassing the family with our presence. It was difficult for Jagat, to leave his work and his beloved home, but there was no option, as we saw it.

"At the end of it, ma said it was okay by her, if it would give me the happiness I sought, but she said she needed time to bring Pa round. But between Dadi and Saloni, where was Pa to ever agree? He never got off his Bhaibund horse and I just had to go right away."

Nina flew back in time, to her escape from the Big House, purportedly with friends for a first day first show new movie.

Instead she had gone straight to one of Jagat's friends who transformed her wild curls into a neat oiled bun. She changed from her pants and top into a blue cotton Puneri *sari* with a patterned border and Kolhapuris and checked into a hotel close by. Even the friends were apprehensive that the family might use police connections to raid their home.

All their fears proved true. The police came and went and then came the news that a watch had been mounted at the railway station and at the airport.

Jagat came up with a new plan. Instead of the Pune-Bombay flight, he put her in one of the Pune-Bombay taxis, to catch the flight to Delhi from Bombay, while he stayed back to put everyone off the trail, as they were looking for Nina with him. A friend booked a ticket at Bombay, under the agreed name 'Ritu Khanna'. The three hour night taxi journey stretched to a nightmarish five hours with a freak storm as soon as they hit the Western Ghats.

Meanwhile her co-passengers were dying of curiosity. They had seen Jagat's loving send off and her obvious nervousness.

"Are you married? Where are you going? To meet the in-laws? Alone?"

Nina made up manfully as they went along. At the Khandala stopover, she almost missed the taxi, talking to Jagat on the phone. He had already confirmed the name of the restaurant where the taxi driver made his regular stopover. He had been dialling frantically for an hour before the taxi drove in. Jagat had been in total panic, fearing the worst when the taxi did not arrive at the stopover at the usual time.

The worst scare came at the Delhi airport, where another friend was meeting her. The public address system blared out "Ritu Khanna, passenger from Bombay please report at the information desk."

Unused to the name, Nina ignored it, not linking herself to 'Ritu Khanna'. In a little while, there was an announcement for 'Nina' and that got through to her. Petrified that her father had traced her, she lurked behind pillars to check the counter. There was a total stranger there. Mustering up her courage, she approached the desk, "Is there any message for Ritu Khanna?" She asked nervously.

The stranger whooped on her. "We were calling out for you for so long. Why didn't you come first?" Nina did not quite know how to answer.

"Where did you go?" Rashmi was not merely curious; she was engrossed in the romance of the tale.

"To my sister-in-law's place."

"What was it like?"

Nina replied back with a smile.

"I can still see it in my mind like a movie, the cute little house, the smell of its various fragrances, of curd in a little *maati khullar*, hot tandoori *rotis*, pickles and *gobhi-aaloo ki sabzi* and Pears soap, all these flavours are always associated with those early days of marriage."

The house belonged to the Railways double-storied quarters going back to the British era. There was a small patio, opening into a smaller drawing room, adjoining a matchbox bedroom. The kitchen led off from the bedroom, with the bathroom behind it and the *aangan* adjoining it. On the other side of the *aangan*, from the kitchen, was the dining room cum store, whatever. It was ditto upstairs. The *aangan* led off to the back entrance, fronted by an open gutter and the back lane. The upstairs did not have that *aangan*. Their stairs rose from the front patio, which was usually the source of eternal neighborhood battles.

But it was amazing what later day occupiers did with these double storied quarters, transforming them into 'elite' homes of substance with velvet sofas and dining room in the aangan to avail of a second bedroom in the store.

"Then? What happened?" breathed Rashmi. Nina gave her a wry smile.

"Do you expect to hear a lifetime story in an hour? We have spent a lifetime together, grown old, raised a family and sent them off into the world. Look, my dear, everyone in this world is entitled to an opinion. But that does not take away the right of each individual to his or her own decisions on how to lead a life. As family, it is for us to leave them to take the decision and then to give them the full support, whether or not we may take a similar decision. Don't forget, no two situations are ever identical. Just as God did not make any two fingers alike, similarly He did not allow identical situations to arise. So each situation has pros and cons of its own and each one of us has to consider that in our own individual lights. Now try and digest what I have told you while I catch up with my sister."

"But Nani must have been giving you news of her."

"That is not the same as actually talking to Nikita, is it?"

"Who would have guessed that after all, your twins would end up with identical dilemmas separated only by the years..." mused Jagat to his mother-in-law, as Nina and Nikita walked out into the garden arm in arm.

*****

10

ANJALI

Everyone looked in wonder. Anjali was certainly a newcomer to the *puja* brigade. Earlier, one occasionally saw her dutifully attending a *satsang* or a two, or appearing at a funeral. But daily, concentrated meditation instead of a fashionable yoga? That too from the woman who had usurped the prized central location of the family Thakurs.

Hardly aware of the gaping mouths and sophisticated raised eyebrows behind her back, Anjali grappled with her own inner demons. She wanted her peace, quiet and relaxation. But the demons would not retreat from her consciousness.

When she closed her eyes, instead of the verdant green of her lawn, she saw the smirks on her sister-in-law, Devi's face almost twenty years ago. She did not even see the dilapidated face that was Devi's today. when she bleated frenetically to Dadi, "What have I done to Anjali that she treats me like this? She invites everyone to her house, except me."

No one answered the question while commiserating with the calculated insult that Anjali had tendered by not inviting her for the *puja* at her house to mark the death anniversary of her husband, Murli.

No one answered because collective memory had not forgotten what Devi herself had done to the self-same Bhabhi since the beginning of the relationship; from small pinpricks like deliberately sabotaging any outing for the newly weds by tagging along everywhere, to picking up her best *saris* without warning, to insulting the new bride's parents with a well practised insolence, calculated, if anything, to destroy any possibility of a cordial sister-in-law relationship.

Not that there was much sympathy for Anjali. She was too beautiful, too self willed, too clever and too self assured to be able to curry sympathy or favour, least of all from her in-laws. These in-laws of hers were the offspring of Ramdada, one of Amma's wealthiest sons, who belonged to the category of Anjali's enemies.

All her life, Anjali had kept them at a distance. After the initial shock over the blatant animosity exhibited immediately after her marriage, Anjali maintained her distance from them. By her own reckoning, her life's biggest achievement was being able to wean her husband from his parents and siblings.

Not that it took very much doing; in fact a more mealy mouthed lot would be difficult to find. It was so much easier to dislike them. Hating them would be to accord them too much undeserved importance. Yet, try as she would, Anjali could not put the past behind her.

Despite the horrific welcome into the family, the new *bahu* had tried to play her role of bhabhi to the two sisters-in-law, as best she could. It was just weeks after her own marriage that the engagement of her younger sister-in-law, Neelu ran into trouble. The original plan of Neelu and Anjali was to proceed on a lengthy tour, of Bangkok, Singapore, Djakarta, Saigon and Manila, culminating in Hong Kong where the marriage was to take place. This was done to avoid some inauspicious elements in the prospective groom's horoscope, during which the two should not meet.

But the plan went awry when her father-in-law succumbed to a sudden heart attack and Anjali's husband Murli was severely ill. Doctors expected him to get worse, rather than better.

All the possible avenues were examined and the *pandits* prescribed a series of *yajnas* and *pujas*, after which the marriage could take place within ten weeks. The aim of the exercise was to distract Neelu who had been the apple of her father's eyes and to prepone the marriage before Murli got worse.

But the would-be mother-in-law was adamant, "There will be no change of plan, rather a period of mourning is a must," she insisted vehemently.

It took all of Murli's and Anjali's tact to deal with the situation of doughty in-laws on one hand, a weepy Neelu and a steely eyed elder sister, Devi pressing her lips ominously at Anjali, for all the world, as if Anjali had stalled the changed plan. More ominous was that glint of the eye which seemed to say silently, "You caused this tragedy in our family, to my father and to my brother."

They had pleaded with the haughty young man, Kumar who was tied to his mama's *pallu*.

"At a time like this, if your fiancé's needs cannot carry more weight for you and become a matter of mere formality, it is definitely time to do a rethink all round. She needs you, just now. After that, the urgency would be gone. If you and your mother want to wait, then we shall wait and observe the full year of mourning, why just some months.

"I am taking this engagement ring into my safe custody. At the end of the year, if both of you still want it, you can take it from me and replace it on her finger. Till then, both of you can feel free to reconsider your positions." Dada spoke wisely.

"That is hardly your decision to take. It is hers, so let her speak," the young man demanded angrily.

"Well, I am speaking," Neelu spoke up, "I think Dada is right."

"So that's settled then. The wedding gets postponed for the time being. It can be held whenever… after one year maybe."

"No, no, no," it was almost a shriek. "That I will not have." Kumar was overwrought.

"Why are you afraid of waiting for a year, now that you've rejected the early marriage offer?" Devi, Neelu's sister demanded angrily.

"*Sab bhool jao*. It is decided now, *beti* first thing tomorrow, we go to the passport office and fill your forms. You're coming to Paris with me," declared Dada.

"Hey what's going on? You can't take her away like this."

"You are not her husband yet. She is our daughter first and foremost. She'll go wherever we please. And she needs to get away from here."

Sixteen months later, barely three months after a grand wedding at Hong Kong, Neelu came back home. Anjali gauged the situation from her sullen looks, "This young woman is ripe for tragedy. What happened to the marriage?" There was no expression of the blooming effervescence of the newly wed but only a sullen solemnity and a brooding look. Gone was the wicked twinkle in her eyes, the acid in her voice, the liveliness of her rallies, where had they all vanished?

The elder brother brooded heavily, as winter crept up, unknown to all but the night watchman. It was only when the cooler was off and the air cooled naturally enough for the need of a coverlet that one knew that winter has arrived. Is marriage a winter too?

Neelu was obviously consumed with a suppressed fury, like that of a woman scorned, waiting to strike at the husband who had cheated her right as a wife, to come first in her husband's affection and as a lover to stand above all else.

And cheated by whom? Not by another woman. That may have been excusable, but by a mother-in-law, that classical destroyer of marital bliss.

She was now ripe for vengeance. In what form will it be extracted?

The retribution had come sooner than expected.

"What happened, ma? Where have I gone wrong? Why does she want to leave me?" This pitiful bleating of the young husband came only after he had spent the better part of an hour pouring vitriol at Murli, Anjali and his mother and raging against a delinquent wife.

"How dare she? Who does she think she is? I'll not tolerate this. I'll ruin her name. I'll not allow her to survive…"

After all those dire threats, suddenly there was a reversal of mood to plead for help, for reconciliation, for a salve to his bruised, eroded ego. He, after all, was husband the great. How could his wife have had the audacity to walk out off his house with bag and baggage in hand, declaring, "Life with you is intolerable, I can stand neither the tension nor the boredom. I just want to move out."

When Kumar threatened for a divorce, she flung his threat back at him by saying, "Who needs a divorce? After this experience, you actually think I want another marriage? Thanks a ton. I've had enough to last a lifetime. Even if you wanted to give a divorce, I wouldn't take it, not just now in any case."

That threw him off balance and he said, "Why? Why not just now?"

"I have my reasons and I'm not bound to tell you. Go right ahead and file for a divorce. It'll take you years, I can promise you."

"But I don't want a divorce, I want you," Kumar changed the track swiftly.

"No, you don't. All you want is a masseuse for your ego and a woman to do for you all that your mother can't or won't do for you. That's all. And I need more than that," she said firmly. "And don't you get physical with me, I'll report to the police, without any hesitation, believe me."

That threat proved to be the last straw. To maintain family peace was a delicate task, undertaken with equal parts of tact, foreboding, anger and pity for the young couple, knowing full well that whatever they did, someone or the other would point fingers and make charges.

The entire family got hooked on, ingeniously splitting up to offer support to both the sides, to Neelu and to her husband, so cleverly that both were taken in. Ultimately it was Dadi, who hammered out reconciliation between the sullen threesome. Neelu, peeved over being outplayed by her mother-in-law, who was resentful at being shown up as the wedge between her son and her *bahu*. The young man himself, got stripped of his self-important smugness and was exposed as a weakling mama's Boy.

"Give it another try," reasoned Dadi. "You cannot give up on marriage just like that. After some time, everyone is able to adjust, *thoda tum karo, thoda woh karegi, thoda aap karenge.*"

Within days, Murli and Anjali went abroad, staying firmly in foreign parts. Eventually it was the tragedy that brought them home. No one knew of the state of Murli's health, except Anjali. And even she did not know too much beyond the spate of colds and fevers and the recurring pneumonia.

"Let's go back to India. It is warmer there. Here it is so cold, the pneumonia is bound to recur time and again," Murli insisted, drawing up plans for a home of their own to counter Anjali's ominous fears. No one was quite prepared for Murli's decision to leave his life abroad.

To stay in India after a lifetime abroad? Was he mad? It must be that wife of his. She was always so strange. See how she never came back to India and did not even produce a child. She must have done some *jadu-tona* on poor Murli...

In vain did Murli explain, "Let me live in peace in my own land. I have had enough of the travel abroad to make money for the family. Let me enjoy that money for a while myself," he had said ruefully.

Yet all looked suspiciously at the extravagance with which he furnished his home, giving in to all those desires he had never dared to lay bare before his parents or siblings, a jacuzzi, a snazzy bar, a heated swimming pool in which he never swam in, sound systems. Anjali got so much into pleasure-seeking. At times, when the carping became shrill and mean, she deflected it from Murli, insisting that it was what she wanted to have. Let them rail at me, she thought. I am immune to them, she felt. But it was not really so, was it?

Anjali had her weak moments too, when she longed, for things which she knew not what or how. One morning, she had returned from her morning walk with a delighted grin on her face.

"You know what I did today?"

Perhaps it was that grin that acted as a damper to his mood. Murli sat down heavily and picked up his paper, "What?"

"I sat on a swing."

"Where?"

"In the garden."

"*Hoon.*" The grump in that response effectively evaporated her grin.

Why, she always ruminated, did women love swings? Isn't it curious that except for the trapeze artists, you never see men on swings? It is always women and girls who are on the swings, in the gardens, the public parks, the playgrounds, the private *jhoolas* at homes, everywhere, all the time, in art, in literature, in songs, in festivals, in the seasons, whatever.

What is the special link between women and swings? She had never given it another thought until that morning.

One morning when she had walked through the almost somnolent garden, a few early walkers and yogasaners, the deserted swings in the children's play area beckoned sensually.

Should she even dare? Even as the two young college girls took advantage of that rare opportunity: has one ever seen a swing in a children's park ever idle, except at 6.30 a.m. in the morning? She had walked determinedly on.

The next day, the area was again deserted. Again the swings beckoned her. Anjali belonged to a family that was totally urban, where the females were repressed into rooms, where there were no gardens, no swings... ever. She could not recall ever sitting on a swing in childhood; except if that massive old world bed mounted on hooks can ever qualify for a 'swing'.

She sat down gingerly on the swing, moving first back and then forward. The sudden loss of equilibrium, with her feet off the earth, shook her. She started to feel conscious, "People must be looking," she thought. Then she consciously decided to ignore the thought.

The first few swings were plain, childlike fun. Then she had aimed higher and while doing so, stretched her arms and put back her head.

She felt the soaring air and was swept by its current. In her line of vision came proud tree tops, touching the sky. It was a balmy, cloudy day; and as yet, no rays of sun had pierced the cloud cover to expose her elation.

Suddenly, she broke free of feeling conscious. "What will people think of is just a self-imposed regulation of time. There's so much to be done still..."

Now she knew, why do only women sit on swings?

It is for that momentary breaking of their eternal bondages. Up there, you are one with the clouds, the birds, and the air. Those velvet lined, gold chains around the ankles are left behind down there, somewhere, as you soar high on your imagination and feel yourself FREE... MOMENTARILY.

All too soon, you're back, with your feet on the earth. The sound of the creaking swings is telling you, "Time's up. Go home."

Is it only the women who need those breaks from the earth-linked bondage, who need that feeling of freedom, no matter how momentarily, when one is linked to no one, tied to no one, dependent on nothing but that little piece of wood underneath and the two ropes holding it up?

The male of the species has created his own world, his own identity and his own rules. The rules that dictate that when she went back a week later, the swings were patrolled by sharp-eyed watchmen even that early in the morning.

In any case, her affair with the swing was over. When she thought about it, the idea of sitting on the swing and reaching the clouds had lost its novelty and was almost scary. Was it because she had reverted to her conditioning? The years of loss of freedom resulted in a fear of freedom, a fear of even the sense of freedom from the pulls of natural and social gravity that the swing represented.

The males of the species have their own freedom. They do not need the crutch of a swing to express or to discover its highs.

Murli and Anjali's house at No. 4 Sanskar Bharti Society was an exceptionally peaceful looking house. To the passerby, it gave off an air of solidity and contentment. Nothing revealed the seething emotions inside.

It was a beautifully proportionate two-storied structure, with gently curving balconies, topped by an ample terrace from which a large solar heater peeped out. A double row of dark glass panes, cut into squares and triangles, rose up the stairwell to the top of the building, like twin eyes of successive sentinels guarding the inhabitants of the house. Was that very fanciful thinking?

A high wall surrounded the corner house, topped with the fencing net which supported the climbing vines. On two sides, the wall was fronted on the road sides by an additional fenced enclosure, supporting the ubiquitous drooping Asoka trees which reinforced privacy.

There were two gates. It was difficult to decide which was the front gate and which was the back as the house was located at a corner. Between the two gates on the inside of the wall, a narrow L-shaped strip of lawn supported a marble sundial. The larger gate opened onto a driveway, which headed into the garage. On the way to the garage, a large double door opened over the shallow steps. It showed off a large T-shaped sitting room, in which both arms were broad, spacious and airy.

To the right of the T's leg was a kitchen that looked out of the garage and the backyard. The dining room was to the right of the kitchen. It opened onto a tiny vestibule and a short walkway leading to the other smaller gate.

Perhaps the most striking feature of the living room was its height – that of its mini atrium proportions going up to the top of the house. A balcony hung around it on both sides. Under the staircase was where the *puja* alcove had once been. The gods and goddesses were later displaced. Where? Where were the Thakurs? Banished from the *puja* nook created for them under the stairs in the drawing room?

Few knew that they had been installed upstairs, in one of the now empty bedrooms. The earlier location was totally central, between the drawing room, the dining and the kitchen. But they faced the entrance door, which made for a poor Vaastu, Anjali had discovered.

Now they were relocated in a simplistic meditation room, with the pride of place not to Laxmi-Narayan, but to Krishna and his Radha, that Liberator of the senses with his life's love, and to Mira who loved him with the exclusivity and devotion that placed her among the very first proponents of Women's Liberation.

Both Radha and Mira revelled in their love and adoration for Krishna, to the point where they even overlooked their marital and worldly ties. And He raised their love to the level of Bhakti and made their names synonymous with devotion. He even made them acceptable to the world at large, as symbols of adoration. No doubt, he was a very pragmatic person who taught the highest order of pragmatism, but above all he spoke for the heart.

There were so many rooms there that the family just assumed that it was for all of them and moved in even while Murli and Anjali were still on vacation, meeting her parents in Gibraltar. Both Neelu and Devi were in residence, along with younger brother Ravi and his family when Murli and Anjali came home to find a full house, with only the master bedroom and the study available to them. Murli was quite ecstatic, "Now for a change, we are all together for a change."

For his sake, Anjali held her peace, despite the daily pinpricks.

Why prepare soup every day for Murli? He looks fine; she is just making him feel ill. That is all she must have fed him for years and that is why he is so ill now.

Eventually Neelu went back home. But Anjali still had Devi and Kavita, Ravi's wife on her hands and a daily dose of ill-will to cope with.

For months, little sound had emanated from the house, but not for a long, long time. Ever since that night long family battle. Even then, only one voice boomed, loud and clear. What had happened that night?

The early morning had seen the arrival of an ambulance. Few days later, the house was immersed in death ceremonies and inundated with mourners. And then came the long silence. What had happened that fateful night?

*****

11

BATTLE FOR THE HOUSE

"Will you and Ravi please shift upstairs for some time? Murli finds it difficult to climb the stairs," Anjali had reasoned with Kavita, Ravi's wife. They were occupying the guest room downstairs, as it gave their kids easy access to the garden.

"Naturally he will, if you do not feed him properly. If you just keep giving him soups and *dal*, instead of some good solid mutton."

"His digestive system can't take that just now. The doctor has laid down a strict diet for him."

"Oh yes, we all know that. That's why you rule the house and the kitchen."

"I rule the kitchen because it is mine. Have I ever ordered the food in your house in Aden?"

"This is our house too. It belongs to the family, doesn't it?"

Anjali was red. She deliberately allowed her voice to rise as she declared ominously, "Let it be very clear. This is my house and I take the decisions here. Yes, I rule. And it is order and rule that you and Ravi shift upstairs, so that Murli need not climb stairs." As she stalked off, Anjali knew that it was not the end of the matter.

Sure enough, the discussion resumed at the dinner table. Ravi was in a nasty mood.

"Murli, you can't tackle stairs. Why don't you and Anjali Bhabhi shift into the old house – it is on the ground floor."

"Isn't this on the ground too?" queried Murli mildly, "I built it that way for my convenience, you know."

"Your convenience only? Not for the family?" The voice rose sharply.

"Meaning?"

"Bhabhi has asked us to vacate our room…"

Murli raised his eyebrows at Anjali.

"I asked Ravi and Kavita to shift upstairs, so you don't have to climb stairs."

"What's wrong with that?"

Kavita and Devi piped up in unison, "She's always giving the orders."

"It's her house. Why not?"

"This house is ours too!"

"Yes, yours too. But primarily it is hers."

Ravi's short temper flared and he banged his fist on the dining table, shouting, "She is an outsider. How can a family property be hers? If it is, then it is Kavita's right as well."

"Kavita has all the rights that Anjali has," maintained Murli equably.

"In fact more," insisted Ravi, "She has produced two sons."

An ashen ghost flitted across Murli's face. Anjali moved to stand behind him, her hand firm on her shoulder. Murli patted her hand and took a deep breath.

"We have several properties. More than one for each one of us. This house is Anjali's." A babble broke out and raged on for some time, before pinpointing the question, "WHY?"

"Because it was built with the money that her father left for her. It is her home and stands in her name."

"How dare you?" The question hung between the two brothers as the wife and the sister held onto Ravi's raised fist. Murli was gasping for breath. As she spoke desperately into her mobile, Anjali was pummeling his chest with her fist with her back to her husband's quarreling siblings. The ambulance took an eternity to arrive – it was too late.

After the final rites were performed, Anjali ensured that the whole extended family was present when she made her announcement. She had earlier won over Dadi to her side by diplomatically taking her in confidence, "Don't you think it will be more peaceful all round if we lived in our own houses and met every week cordially, instead of living together and fighting all the time?"

Now she addressed Ravi, "Your father left a lot of property, enough to take care of the entire family. You are now in charge of it."

Ravi looked discomfitted perhaps with the new burden of responsibilty and Devi patently belligerent. Until now, she had handled all the properties, their rentals, fixed deposits, investments etc.

"Murli and I built this house for ourselves, from my money. No-one else has any right to it," she paused significantly and then continued, "You are all welcome as guests. I will make no demands on your properties. I have my own money from my father and Murli's insurance. If not, I'm sure my brother can afford to feed me."

Dadi spoke up with tight lips, "*Naak katwaigi kya hamari?* My brother had earned enough to feed seven generations.

Why should your brother feed you? Ravi, you and Devi sit with Anjali and decide how much she needs every month for daily expenses. But," she enquired worriedly, "what are you going to do with this huge house all by yourself?"

"We had planned lots of things which didn't happen as he had so little time and he was surrounded by the family. Now I will plan again." Her look became steely.

Anjali's renovations took a long while. She had learnt patience. She waited throughout the long year of mourning, staying tactfully in Dadi's shadow, yet maintaining her personal distance. The long spells of loneliness were broken by her various siblings, her sisters, cousins, brothers, bhabhis and parents who took turns to make extended visits. Anjali did not visit her London *maika* until after the formal year of mourning and the attendant rituals were finally over.

While she spent a well earned vacation touring Europe and America with her sister, the workmen took over the house, implementing the plans she had discussed in full detail. Neelu and Devi, Dadi and Ravi paid visits to the Sanskar Bharti house and queried the contractor, but the poor man only knew what the interior designer had ordered.

The guestroom downstairs remained there only but one of the rooms upstairs was converted into a kiddies' den. For whom? Another bedroom upstairs had the bed and the cupboards taken out, replaced by large round tables and sitting areas, opening onto a generous sit out with... was that a bar? Other guestrooms, one with handrails for elderly use and a room left totally blank except for a beautiful marble central platform and carved niches at intervals on the side and an elaborate music system. What was Anjali planning?

The interior designer had a mind of her own and a brief from Anjali, "I am sending her photographs as the work progresses.

And she has approved of what has been done. Why do you worry?" The designer demurred.

Finally, Anjali returned after six months. This time, the house warming party was a subdued one. "Without Murli, I don't feel like it," she demurred to all and sundry.

Several doors remained locked. She explained to Dadi, "The guestrooms are for whoever comes. I have planned a special room for their children, so the parents can have privacy when they come here. Why not, with such a big house and so many rooms? And the special room upstairs is for my parents or for you, whenever you come to stay with me."

What about the banished Thakurs, thought Dadi. Where were they? Anjali put her mind at rest. "See my meditation room."

The Thakurs had been relocated in a simple meditation room, with the pride of place given not to Laxmi, but again to Krishna and his Radha, The others lived in the niches around the room. Soft music and *bhajans* flooded the senses.

What about the room with the bar, the tables and the sit out?

But before Anjali could embark on her own new life, she had odds and ends to finish off, a dispute that was left simmering decades ago. That of Neelu and Kumar which was patched up by Dadi. Now Neelu was back, frothing at the mouth and demanding freedom.

"Neelu, how can you leave him now? You have your kids to see to and you know Kumar has not done well at all; not enough to give you anything like a decent settlement. What will you do?"

"What will I do? If my father's properties can look after you, why not after me and my children?"

"That is not the point. Marriage or rather, divorce is not about the settlement alone, is it? What about your lives which you have lived together and now separate? The effect on the children?"

"Forget it bhabhi. I don't care. But I will not let him get off scot free, to do the same things to someone else what he has done to me. I'm going to screw him."

"But how? What sort of a case can you make out in the court, when you have lived with him all these years and he has looked after you and the children as well as he could?"

"And how well was that? With his constant battles with bosses and changing jobs? If it weren't for my brothers, he would be out of jobs and my kids would be starving."

Dadi spoke up, "Go to a good lady lawyer and tell her you have been married for thirteen years and your husband has made you and the children change ten homes because he has changed twelve jobs. See what she has to say," she declared astutely.

*****

12

CARD ROOM CONFIDENCES

The mysteries of Anjali's renovations emerged very gradually, as she slowly picked up the threads of her life back home. Yoga, yes, a teacher came in twice a week to work with her. Meditation was also a part of her routine, along with long sessions at the beauty parlour.

This had sprung up almost overnight in the little outhouse in a corner of her property, giving her an in-house beautician, a smart woman.

But regular as clockwork that yoga and beauty care was, more regular were the cards, a passion shared with a motley crew, some family members, some young, some not so young and some old. Everyone brought in friends to the regular card sessions.

Once in a while, the sessions took on a different stance. This time, after the others left, there were still a handful left, all family *bahus*, *betis*, nieces, not yet ready to go home, even though they had had their fill of the cards session.

A dangerous mood prevailed.

The dissatisfaction habitual on the face of Mohini, Dadi's only daughter had taken a slightly lighter cast today, as if she was enjoying a secret. She did not even take offence once at being addressed as *Moti* (Fatty).

"Come on now. Tell us and you will enjoy it more," teased Anjali.

"What is there to enjoy? Some plus, some minus; my life has more minus than plus." Moti started off on her usual self-pitying plaint, overlooking how she blackmailed money out of everyone on the sound premise that the 'family' owed her. Mohini had had the original failed NRI marriage; she flew to the United States to find that they had married her to a man that was already-married-to-a-Firang.

Watching the dying-of-curiosity faces, she declared gleefully, "Okay Baba, I'll tell. That *naalayak* son of mine, Kunal... for three years now, I'd put up with his girlfriend, Urvashi practically living in, and out of his bedroom totally shamelessly. I thought *chalo, kamau bahu milegi.*"

"What happened? That idiot used to do nothing but *udao* money in failed projects, while she worked in some computer company. Urvashi saw him loafing when he should have been at work, they had a big fight and she walked out from his life. Now he's gone into Devdasgiri, with a beard and all."

"What I can't understand," interposed Prema, one of the family *bahus*, "is why you tolerated it in the first place?"

"What to do, my dear? What to do? Throw out my only son? Are you mad? They are at that age when they want such things and the girls are willing to give everything nowadays. Who wants to wait for a marriage and all its hassles? See, my dear, this was plain and simple *jism ki bhookh*. It's like servicing which the machines need. The body is also a machine, isn't it?"

"What about your body?"

"It had its needs also. Did I ever look like a dried out prune? Actually I feel I am bloating now because of lack of servicing. You all know how I had fought with my mother to shift to that flat away from the Big House. Why do you think I shifted in the first place? Away from all those crones? The trick is how to get what one wants."

"How did you manage that?"

"Arrey Baba, by hit and miss. I used to call friends home for drinks and pot luck. All sorts of friends and all sorts of pot luck. If something worked out, fine. But no regulars. *Bahut lafda karte hain.* Who wants that sort of a hassle?"

"Suppose some unwanted person showed up?"

"My house is always open to neighbours, friends, their kids, servants etc. If I don't want him and he still shows up, he's drowned in drinks and kids, the more the merrier. He'll not know how to handle it. I only shoo everyone out when I want to, no? And then a woman can get periods and has to do *pujas* and visit relatives etc. It usually works."

"And if you get pregnant?"

"No chance, baby. Right in the beginning, after Kunal, I made friends with the doctor and got a laparoscopy done. So no *chinta.*"

"But *Moti,* there are other health problems in this..."

"Why worry so much? I am clean and openly ask them also – *Bindaas,* up front – *AIDS vaids to nahi hai, baba?* And if someone chooses to tell a lie, we all have to die some time. Suppose that bastard I married had given me AIDS from his American bitch?"

"So now?"

"Now what? Kunal's stuck at home all day. Anyways, I'm going on a trip with my friends." (Everyone had their own quota of 'friends', unique to them, real or imaginary, who were strictly non-family, non-Sindhi.)

"How come?"

"A group tour. They go every year. This time I'm going also. Fifteen ladies, some are singles and the others getting away from their husbands. One has a mother-in-law along, but the old lady's totally *Bindaas*, like me."

"How will the all woman show solve your problem?"

"Arrey Baba, why are you so hung up on that? It is a hit and miss, my dear, no big deal. So many tours, so many groups, so many stop overs, *kuch ho bhi sakta hai*. If not, I'm not that desperate. Traveling and company is good enough for me. *Phir* Mata will also give me something, no? I sing nice *bhajans*."

"How will you pay for the trip? You're always running short."

"Mama Naval is going to pay for the tour. I told his wife who told him, "*Mata ne bulaya hai, to jaana parta hai.*" And if Anjali will deal me some good hands, my shopping will be taken care of."

"Which Mata is this?"

"Vaishno Devi," Mohini *Moti* rolled her eyes wickedly as the group broke up in laughter, knowing that the Maami could never resist a pilgrimage, even someone else's.

"What about Kunal?"

"What about him? The *bais* will cook and clean the house. One of you keep tabs on him and hopefully, by the time I come back, he'll be bored of the *Devdas* routine and will be dying for another girl."

Prema was not amused at all, "How can you take things so lightly?"

"How heavily to take them? *Bolo*? I have no husband, so should I become a *sadhvi*? Bull shit!! If a woman dies, everyone starts hunting for an another woman for him; '*Bechara*, how will he live? Manage the children alone?' But no one thinks like that when a man dies or walks out. We have to manage, somehow. Then, when I talked of taking a job, the Mama's bloody noses got involved. So, fine, I didn't take that job. They have to feed us then. And why should I only be on short rations because the husband they found for me was a bastard? You go for holidays with your husband. What about me? I can chat online at home, but I also want to get away sometimes."

"Don't talk of holidays," said Prema with a shudder. She swallowed nervously. This was thinner ice than she had ever skated before, even with her in-laws. Everyone put down their cards. "Come on," said Anjali, "Confession time for all. For once, let's all let our hair down and learn about each other's feelings and problems, in-laws and out-laws. Here, let's be friends first and then relatives."

Moti exploded, "That's the problem. One can speak to friends. But relatives? Ask yourself."

It was Laajjo who spoke first, "Friends, relatives, what does it actually matter? Everyone is entitled to a personal option. Only don't thrust it down someone else's throat. I've been through the mill too, after the sisters left and the club began to lose its attraction. So I took a job. Mine were regulars – three bosses in a row. No one thought of it when I was widowed so young. So what option did I have, husbands of my *nanads*? They had itchy hands; thank God they went off abroad soon. So there I was, holding an excellent job, on paper; in fact, at home, on short holidays, long conferences, whatever… my mother-in-law knew about it, how could she not when they used to come home for dinners, and stay on till late? So did Dadi – I think – but she never brought it out openly."

"And then?" there was a ripple of curiosity and sympathy.

"My Sonu died in a boarding school picnic disaster. Suddenly it came to me, what was I making all that money for? For whom? Around the same time, my mother-in-law also passed away; and I went bonkers. We had built up a stable relationship of loving and bitching. I even tried to commit suicide, but I was too much of a coward to do it properly."

"Then…"

"My last boss was a big piece of shit. He felt that constant sex was the only way out of an emotional trauma, all day, night, everywhere, office, home, club and Lonavala company guest house."

"No one found out?"

"The whole office knew. But he got careless and his wife found out."

"And… divorce?"

"No way. She knew her man. And his worth in the long run. So did I. Their kids were young then. I struck a deal with her; between us, we took him to the cleaners. Each of my bosses had given me shares so I had a big chunk. I unloaded all that on him and took solid property as a lump sum settlement along with cash in the form of VRS. And she got him in a big hook for the rest of her life. If only *aurat aurat ki dushman na hoti, to bahut kuch hota.*"

"I completely agree," declared Veena, another of the *bahus* emphatically, "But you could only do all this, believe me, because you were not emotionally handicapped by that terrible *paon ki bedi* called a 'husband'. Just think back. If you had a husband, would you have gone to work, made money and lived as you pleased? All around me, I see single women living well and… ask me, my daughter, Shimoli is working, but how much does she make and what does it get spent on?"

"What, *bolo na?*"

"She used to work before marriage and have a ball, but gave up that job to go abroad with her husband. When she wanted to work there, he made such a *hungama*… I am the breadwinner, you will save your money, not spend it etc. Within months, he was planning what luxuries it could be spent on. In no time, they were fighting, whether to spend it on her luxuries or his!!

"Now her money is spent faster than his salary and more than half of the fights are over money. Sometimes, I think the old way was better when we ladies lived here and the men abroad. We didn't know what exactly they were up to, so it didn't hurt us. And what they sent, gave scope for some luxuries over and above the necessities, so we were contented – rather than this constant slow simmer, which only ends with a divorce."

"Veena, your husband just got back last year after almost twenty years. Don't tell me you are fed up already?"

Veena looked around at her audience. There was a long pause and then they felt that she was choosing her words with extreme care. Soon they knew why.

"I don't know. Honestly I have not been able to make up my mind whether I was better off without him around at all. I lived in India with my kids, not rich but comfortable. I left him in South Africa because he had a woman there and I refused to accept that. Since the kids were with me, he had to make proper provisions. Actually," it came out slowly, thoughtfully, "we used to have good fun, the kids and I, making do with whatever he sent. Without him around, they were a bit wild at times, but that was inevitable, wasn't it?"

The question was rhetorical, "Yes, I do remember occasionally thinking of the sex. How much does a wife get when the kids are already around and there is another woman in the picture? He was quite the handsome hero before I landed there. My appearance must have upset quite a number of his *bijlis* and he resented that very much. But things settled down after he accepted that he was a family man. One after another, the kids came along, but when I discovered that there was this steady female, I blew my top and left, for good."

"What brought him home now?"

"So many things. The kids grew up and the boys went to South Africa. They sent me enough money to move into the luxury bracket and they worked on him too, I suppose. Then that woman fell ill and left. He came home when Shimoli got married; then he fell ill and stayed put, maybe because she was not there waiting for him. And I had him on my hands," she finished laconically.

"You don't sound too happy about it."

"*Haal mat puchho.* I'm not used to having a man around all the time, asking what you are doing, why you are doing that. Where are you going, why, what to cook, what to wear, Baba… it is terrible. I used to live as I pleased. To go or not to go anywhere was my decision. Now he wants to go everywhere and I have to go with him, just to keep the peace. Sometimes, I feel he just wants to show off to the world that he has got me, in spite of everything."

There was another long pause, as if Veena was wondering whether to go further in baring her soul. Then she started off again, "I was not used to physical sex. *Nahi to nahi hota hai yaar*, what's the big deal? But now, every night, sometimes, all night, oh my god, I get so tired. Then he had the audacity to accuse me by saying, 'You put me off', and showed me what she used to give him, XXX CDs, he called it *Angrezi Kamasutra*. I yelled back at him, 'What have you ever done for me not to put you off? I've taken enough punishment for my parents' mistake in marrying me to you and my mistake in bearing your kids. Now you want me to be your whore? Go to Hell,' I told him. Actually sex is good fun, sometimes, even many times. But all the time? Like a bloody pumping machine?"

Veena shuddered at the thought. "I kept thinking what to do to chase him right back where he came from, so I could have some peace."

The audience was stunned. This mouse Veena, the gossip, the ever ready table filler and party and *puja* help, with such strong feelings?

"Don't look at me like that. I mean it and I did it."

"How?"

"I got her email address from my sons. It turned out that she had fallen ill and the doctors had told her to stop sex. He was eyeing her niece and she put her foot down and walked out. That's how they split up. Then she got better and missed all their hectic sex. After all they had had a relationship for over twenty years. She beckoned and I pushed and he went right back. QED.

"Just imagine, if he had stayed on, I would have ended up falling sick myself. And why should I do that to myself for a man who did not stand by either me or my children? Did anyone of you ever guess what had happened in my life? Always, I have kept a false façade of cheerfulness, for the sake of the kids. Otherwise I would have ended up in a lunatic asylum and where would my children have been then?"

"The family would have looked after them," Prema was sarcastic, "Why are you all so hung up on sex? Is there nothing else to marriage?"

"You tell us what else there is. I am tired of it Baba. I used to be so comfortable, wearing what I felt like, once a month at the parlor for something something. Here all day he would be after me, paint my nails, asking me to put on lipstick and eye shadow, brush my hair, dye my hair, wear high heels, shop for the latest things, lingerie, do this, do that, for all the world as if I was preparing to get married, instead of preparing to die!"

"*Arrey mare tere dushman.* Veena darling, there is more to marriage than sex and just looks."

"Tell us, na, you've had a long marriage too and just come back after living years in Panama, without Sanjay in tow as usual. What's happened?"

"What could happen? *Bas nazar lag gayi.* We celebrated our silver anniversary in grand style, because no one had expected that our marriage would last so long, with Sanjay's mother always so dead set against me, plus no kids," Prema revealed.

"It had been a rough ride," she continued, "She thought I was secondary to her because we were not Bhaibunds and on top of that, I did not give her any grandchildren, not even a daughter. Sanjay and I had a perfect understanding. We lived life as we wanted. When we came here, I kowtowed to his mother and family. When we went to my family, he did the same to them and then we went off on our own holidays. After some time, it became a strain when the kids did not appear. I went through the whole charade of doctors, treatments, *pujas* and the works, but how could I produce a child when it was Sanjay who refused to take the treatment he needed."

There was a long pause and then a strange new reality poured out, "Actually we had gotten used to our life as we were leading it. Plus his responsibilities to his family which his elder brother, Sunil sidestepped because he had a handicapped child. And what we saw of the intrusions and upheavals caused by the kids did not quite help. Sunil's wife, Sunita, was a total bitch. She left the child to servants who kept him filthy and hungry. Until I went there, he only got attention when guests came. Otherwise she never talked to him or taught him anything. I know because I looked after him. But if anyone came and I handled him, she would insult me and keep repeating, *'apna baccha hota to jaanti'.* So we decided, *'nahi to na sahi.* If God did not will it, then why force it?'

"But that decision was our secret. His ma did not know and we knew that she would never be able to accept or understand, so we did not tell her. Having a secret to share became a bond which held us through all the ups and downs of our life. No one could ever understand that.

"Of course, it created problems, that too, big ones. Sanjay's reaction was to take such interest in food that he became a gourmand; he would hog and hog and I would collapse making food for him. You've seen his belly. No restaurant could open without his being there to sample their stuff and offer his opinion to the critics who had come. And he ran through the menus of all the restaurants in Panama City. It came to such a stage that I would throw up and be unable to eat, just thinking of all that food. The doctor told us that it was an allergy, but what the hell. Seeing so much food makes any ordinary person sick."

"Then what happened? Why did you come back?"

Pain flitted across Prema's face. Her life flashed past, the wonderful times, the togetherness, the caring for each other. At what stage did that collapse? Was it the food thing? Or the lack of kids? Or did his mother finally get through to him? Where did they go wrong?

"I confess, at times I did get so fed up of her attitude that I used to corner him with 'her or me'. But Sanjay was wonderful. He balanced both of us and I would feel sorry for being bitchy and start being extra nice to her. But, I suppose everything takes its own toll. There I was holding onto my husband, in spite of ma's hostility and no kids to cement the bond.

"And when I fell really ill, I had to go to my parents' place for a long time to recover. We could not call Ma to Panama; she did not like that place and she was too old to do much in any case. And he was all alone there, while I was supposedly 'holidaying', if it can be called that, with my parents!! *Bas to kya tha.* Stag nights and all night drinking-eating binges, the Internet and its pornographic seductions."

"What???"

"Yes. All those years of being together, of caring and loving, of eating and not eating and everything flew out of the window.

He hardly replied to my emails. By the time I got back, I found myself shut out, a stranger in his life who got barked at for intruding between him and his Net friends. I told him he was old enough to be father to those sluts, but it had no effect. We barely exchanged a word all day, apart from meals. Now I knew how his Ma must have felt when I walked into his life and she had to take the back seat. How we had hated each other! Now I sympathise with her. She's ill. That's why I have come to look after her since she hates Panama."

"And Sanjay?"

"He'll come and go. Let's see how long this infatuation lasts. Don't forget he is past middle age. All this will definitely affect his health. But it is no use saying so. Let him discover it himself from the doctors, without me around. That's the only way to knock sense into him. Meanwhile..."

"Why don't you just drop him?"

"After a lifetime together? We loved each other a lot. And it is still there. It just needs time to surface. I have not lost faith. Maybe being with Ma will be my penance. But then who knows, *kal kya ho kisne jaana*? How many times over and over again does a man demand a loyalty test of his woman, while he himself fails in all such tests miserably? Willy-nilly a choice is forced down a woman's throat – your family or mine, they demand a total wrenching out of the umbilical cord while they cling to their own cords.

"I noticed one thing about the families with kids. Initially the children are father's, *mera baccha*. Only when they do something wrong, they become mother's, *tera baccha*. And then they demand another choice, which includes either they are your children or mine.

"When the chickens come home to roost over the accumulated neglects of decades of growing up, and they cannot connect with the children, they sit nursing their sulks and the women, correct me, if I am wrong, have to start adjusting to a new set of circumstances, children going away and husbands coming back home. In your daughters you see what you yourselves were a quarter of century ago, you see your own hopes and despairs being reflected there. And in your sons, you see your guys; that is why you want to tell them '*Saalo*, if I had had all these privileges, lord knows where I would have been today'.

"At the bottom of his heart, I know Sanjay does love me still, but the daily scrubbings have worn the skin thin and tender and the relationship has become acerbic. So one treads carefully, as one treads on dreams. I'm giving him time and myself too."

"Did you never think of the adoption option, when you could not have a kid, as it was affecting both of you so much?"

"Of course, it was very much there on our minds. First we had convinced ourselves that we were happy as we were, accepting God's will. Then there was a prolonged battle. Sanjay's mother wanted us to adopt from the family and my parents from theirs. We even thought of a third option, but no one would accept an adoption from outside. They felt one does not know what sort of blood will come into the family. But the problem with a family adoption is that any time the real parents or siblings may demand recognition and then where would I be? Sunil's wife used to leave her son entirely to me but when guests come, she would insult me if I even came into the room. I did not want a family adoption and so that was that. Fortunately Sanjay supported me on that, so Ma had to lay off, but it was held against me for a long time."

"*Satya vachan. Kal kya ho kisne jaana*? This whole in-law thing is very tricky, no one can get a handle on it," Laajjo declared.

"I thought you had your in-laws well in hand now."

"Those Lata and Rita, as soon as they came back last month they have been on my back, asking who gave me the right to do charity in their mother's name! I gave it back to them with interest, asking 'How dare you ask me what right I have to do charity in your mother's name? Who are you to question that?'

"When their father fell ill, they plotted and planned to make me the scapegoat for hospital duty so they could do their social service bit. After marriage, they fled abroad, leaving their old mother with me. When she fell ill, I looked after her, till she died. Where were they then? Now they have no right to ask any questions about my relationship with her.

"After her death, no one ever came forward to ask me what was happening in my life, or whether I had any problems, after the double loss of Sonu and her. I did what I wanted to, set up a trust in their names, from which I paid for the education of poor children in my old school. They just wanted to grab their father's and brother's insurance money, which were already in the trust.

"They shouted, 'How dare you do charity in our mother's name? Why do such a weird thing?' What was weird about giving some poor children an education? There should have been big battles over the weird things I had done, taken a job, slept with other men after my husband died and then gave it all up when my son died. I told them to shoo off because I was a weird person, so be it! I told them I was more her daughter than them, so I had the right to do charity in her name, not them."

"Good grief, I never knew Lata and Rita were that money-minded. Everyone thinks they are saints dressed in white," said Veena.

"We are better off in coloureds, believe me. White is nothing but a sham. Sometimes I feel that these young people who are so *bindaas* are better; *jitna chala, chala.* Then good bye… as long as there is no kid to mess up things."

"My Guruji says it is easy to debunk marriage as a rotten bond but what to replace it with?" demanded Mohini, "One speaks disparaging about the women who cling to marriage only because they worry about who'll pay the bills and who'll support them and the kids. Is this not the pragmatic approach for one who is fettered with children and has no family fortune to fallback on, a loving mother, smitten by a wayward husband, to give total social and economic support at home, plus money in the bank? Everyone cannot be a dedicated career woman who will make good, no matter what – without the casting couch or the godfather?"

"Isn't that also being judgemental?" interposed Naina, Vasudev's daughter who had been listening all this while. "Who are we to judge those who need the godfather or the Gurujis, *satsangs* and *bhajans* or a laptop to maintain their equilibrium? Do you know what is happening in Saloni's life with a husband out of sight and out of mind and a daughter who ran away to become a model; or Sheila's who lost two children one after another to drugs? Why go far? What about my life? I am not into *satsang* yet, but I have started doing yoga. You know why? Just to find some peace, if I can.

"Yes, question me. What is my problem? Life had its ups and downs but I coped. Then what happened? An accident took one child and the rest have gone off to lead their own lives. I spent my whole life for the kids and now they are gone and I am left alone. I know they are doing well and are – happy with whatever they are doing. Yes, they do have problems; but can anyone go through life without problems? They have to cope, otherwise how will they learn? Wouldn't life be totally boring without something to overcome, something to achieve, especially for today's youngsters who want so much from life?

"All that is very well. I want it for them. But what about me? I wanted something, more than just the TV, the cards and the company of my husband, who is so happy in his retirement. Like Veena, getting used to having him on my hands all the time, after having lived together only occasionally. I know what I want, my children with me, cannot be. So there is just this strange loneliness but not aloneness, which I have to combat. So I do yoga for mental peace. Tell me, am I crazy or weird?"

They sat absorbing the respective revelations. Guna spoke up. She was Naina's sister, one of youngest family *betis* who never married. At this point of time, few could recall why it happened that way. But it had and Guna was the classic spinster, with a cold heart and an acid tongue.

She couldn't bear to be alone, yet could not bring herself to live with her own sister or her bhabhi who had moved into plush flats in town. So her life was spent in the Big House and in looking after the family properties, *satsang,* friends and relatives' visits to pass time, not without some acrimony. Her words were a surprise, "*Zindagi ka nazariya kaise badalta hai*? Suddenly we are the older generation – going for the morning walks, even slow walking tires me out. I do only light work at home, cutting vegetables, *seva* of *thakurs* etc, that is a therapy. Last week, after a long time, I found myself in a small garden, in the company of people are – ordinary people, just people. Young mothers bringing their kids to a garden, gaggles of kids only talking to those they knew, not making friends, just like the grown ups. Tension loomed large on parents' faces, mostly mothers, with a sprinkling of fathers. Only two categories are relaxed, the two or three grandpas who were not worried about going home to do evening chores or cooking. And the other were the servant girls, released from *bhaisaheb's* overlooking, enjoying a quiet relaxation and a gossip session amidst the noise."

Geeta, another of the Big House girls, had been listening quietly in a corner. Now she came forward to speak up. "I have spent a lifetime in marriage. We never thought anything of the adjustments we had to make or the nonsense we had to take. But it is different now. Look at my five children. Pritam married Sonia, whom we selected for him. Sonia loved her social life and in the beginning Pritam indulged her. As his responsibilities in business and at home grew, he started going slow on the party front, which he used to do for Sonia's sake. Things reached to such a stage that she divorced him. I know he is seeing some one else, but I am waiting for him to tell me himself.

"The second son's wife makes him dance nicely to her tunes and he loves it. Seeing that made Rahul, a professional, insist that he would marry a professional girl only. So he married one. He plunked everything on her shoulders, home, children, taxes, bills, banking, everything. If she asked him to do anything on those fronts, he sulked. So naturally when he insisted that he should decide where they should invest their money or go for a holiday, she sulked. After all they had been equal partners. Because they were busy with their careers, they had a limited social life. But if she had to go for her office evenings, whether mixed or ladies sessions, he sulked. Whenever they are on the verge of a blow up, I bring the kids over to my place and let them handle each other.

Seeing her brothers, and bhabhis' affairs, my daughter Khushi insists that she will only marry whenever she finds Mr. Right. And since he has not come along yet, she is happily single, with herself and her friends, doing what she wants."

*****

13

PINOCCHIO

We took Maya's ashes to Haridwar. It was quite a family outing, or rather a ladies' outing, commanded by Dadi and an assortment of others. Gunwant begged off and for the compulsory need for a male to fix taxis etc, we took along our cook Ramu.

On the train to Delhi, Lavina asked, "Where will we stay?"

"In the *ashram* guest house."

"What *ashram*?"

"There is an *ashram* known to us. Dadi Hari lives there. We've sent a telegram to reserve the rooms for us."

"Who is Dadi Hari?" They recognised the persistent questioning.

"One of our family members. She and Sita decided to live in Haridwar after Partition. Sita died some time ago."

"How?" Dadi began to lose her temper.

"How? I don't know. Ask Hari when you meet her, if she speaks to you. She always tries to ignore us as if we are inferior to her and she is the Partition heroine." The tone was a giveaway to deep resentment.

The trip by road from Delhi to Haridwar was an eye opener on how things were changing, large expanses of good road and

American style motels punctuated by bone shaking stretches of potholes. At places, the potholes in the roads were eased by the sugarcane bagasse spread out to dry on the road, accompanied by the noxious odour of perhaps a thousand distilleries.

The roads were lined with massive hoardings advertising all manners of agricultural equipment, from tractors to pump sets and white goods, from food processors to washing machines, all expensive energy guzzlers. Asked about the apparent popularity of the washing machines, the driver revealed, "*Aji memsaab*, when there is power in the mornings, first the machine is used to churn milk; after *Bebe* has her supply of butter and *lassi*, it is washed out and then the clothes are put in… if there is still power then."

We arrived past noon, descended on the *ashram* guesthouse and were escorted to our rooms. "Dadi Hari is in meditation," the manager said. Everyone accepted it with equanimity. The older women settled in to sleep off their fatigue. Lavina excused herself. Across the road were the temples, spacious, airy, cool, and serene.

She wondered, "Where is Dadi Hari? Why did she not meet us? After all, it is natural when someone comes from home, isn't it?"

Dadi Hari was sitting, crouched over her knees in a solitary corner. She had a troubled round face. A grandmotherly figure in plain stark long-sleeved white blouse and *sari*, she looked every inch the loving grandma, except for that troubled look on her face. She must have sensed a presence after some time. Her eyes opened. They exchanged courtesies.

"Why?" Lavina's eyes were a mute question. "Why did you never come home?"

"This is my home now."

"You know what I mean. The whole family is there. You are alone here."

It took a long while to break down the wall of silence around the horror she had lived with for decades. The horror that befell the beautiful Sita and her little sister Harini and to recall that was painful. As Lavina listened, she could only hope that it was cathartic as well.

*****

Sita and Harini were tailing Rajjo-rani, the beautiful *Mussalmaani* whom Baba had not married. They had heard the old story and it was the *dhoban* who had pointed Rajjo-rani out to Sita. Tailing her was a great fun, she visited all the grand shops, shopping for jewellery, *dupattas*, bangles, and *mojris*. Then what happened?

Suddenly a huge black blanket enveloped them and they were loaded on a cart. Sita clutched her little sister's hand, holding her as she fainted. When Harini woke up, they were in a cellar. The only light was the moonshine from a window at the top of the stairs. Mice rolled over the blanket covering them.

Some men came to take Sita. They were saying, "Their family thought Rajjo was not good enough for them. Let's see what their girl is worth."

Those were the wild days when the winds of Partition were raging and there was no law except that of might. Women were the first casualties. Abduction was a norm.

When they dragged Sita up, a foot came down on Harini's leg and she shrieked with pain. "Arrey, here's another one. A babe, why did you bring her? She's useless." But Sita would not let go of Harini's arm and dragged her along with her.

What would have happened if Sita had left Harini there?

Upstairs, they were led to the *zenana*, cleaned up and separated. Sita was taken away, forcibly. When she came back, she could barely walk. She looked strange and smelt strange. She slept and slept. When she woke up, she was called away again. Again, she could barely walk when she came back, she smelt strange and she slept like the dead beside Harini.

After some time (was it days or weeks?), they were enveloped in black again and taken to another place. Different faces, different looks, but shabbier people. The treatment was the same. Sita went away all evening and night and slept all day.

After the third change of place, slowly Sita regained her cheer. In fact, she was more cheerful, she sang songs and twirled on her toes, maids applied henna on her hands and oiled her hair, massaged her body in the day. Sita quickly reverted to her earlier self, recovering her striking looks, doe eyes, gay moods and spicy tongue although there were no bhabhis here to rail at or set against each other. She even got some beautiful clothes to wear. Sita explained carefully to Harini, "Shahji is a big man. He'll look after us." But although she took care to see that Harini was well fed, she also took pains to ensure that the little one was cleaned or oiled or put into pretty clothes.

One day, an old *Dai* took Harini in hand, bathed her, oiled and plaited her hair and put on a clean outfit. The child raced off with her playmates and found herself in a new part of the *haveli*. She caught the fancy of the wrong eyes immediately. The children ran about the huge *haveli* and landed in a private chamber, Shahzada's, who had an eye for pretty children.

"Come play with me and I'll tell you stories," he called. "Who is this pretty little girl? Have you heard of Pinocchio?" He launched into an artful rendition of the Pinocchio fable, signalling the boys to take off their clothes. They obeyed.

"Come my pretty one, if you want to play with us, you have to take off your clothes."

Harini demurred. What strange people were these? At home, they were never allowed to remove all their clothes altogether, not even when they bathed. And here... but Shahzada did the honours and placed her on his lap as he continued with his tale, "...and his nose grew longer and longer and redder and redder," he said dramatically.

"How can that be? That's a tale like that of *bhoots*," cried Harini.

"It's true. See Dholu's thing. You rub your hands on it. If he has told lies it'll grow big."

Harini looked up at the Shahzada round-eyed. "Try it." He pulled Dholu forward and propelled her hands. His little manhood refused to rise to the occasion.

"See, he tells the truth. But not Sheikhu, try him." Sheikhu was older and Harini was wide-eyed. Now came Shahzada's trump card.

"Want to see how many lies I told?" His nostrils flared as he laid back, his beady sunken eyes on the little one perched on her knees between his legs. As she rubbed, it rose and rose in length and breadth. Harini was awestruck.

"Shahzade, such lies!" She breathed.

"Punish me." Her eyes blinked in his direction. "Sit on it and jump on it till it goes back. That is the punishment for telling lies."

The little one was totally dazed and uncomprehending. Then her mouth was an open 'O' of pain and wonder as the Prince lifted her up, fitted himself into her and propelled her up and down. What was greater, her agony or his ecstasy?

Someone popped something into her mouth and after a while, she felt she had left her body. It was only later, when the *Dai* massaged her that the pain and the soreness appeared. The *Dai* put her to sleep with a drink of hot-spiced milk.

Sita was busy and totally unsuspecting. She did not know that night or any of the following nights about what happened in the afternoons, the games of Pinocchio and the leapfrog that

Shahzada played with naked children. The day Harini caught fever, Shahzada was fed up. He rode off, leaving word to send her away and Harini was packed off to – after all, who would take soiled goods – a *dhobi*.

However, the child was oblivious to what she had been through – except for the initial pain and soreness. For three days, the *dhobi* nursed Harini in his little hut, the last in the *dhobi* lane on the outskirts of the village.

On the fourth day, she was able to get up, walk to the river for a proper bath and drink some strong sweet tea. All day, she remained indoors, working, resolutely cleaning and cooking. However, when the *dhobi* approached her that night, Harini was very much the little lady.

"You are only a *dhobi*. Don't touch me," she commanded imperiously.

"You little slut. For days, I tended you – you were not averse to my touch then. Now I'll make a *dhoban* of you. Put a little *mussalman dhobi* in your belly too," he slung roughly at her as he pinned her down and raped her repeatedly. The next day she was locked in after he was done with her, cruelly, maliciously.

When the *dhobi* came back in the evening, he was accompanied by two others, a blacksmith and a potter, all roaring drunk. "This is my *shahzadi* – tonight she is all yours," he declared grandly.

Harini's life was a nightmare, with her captor determined to punish her with all the manner of drunken, coarse, stinking menials every night. Little did they know that the rescue squads from India roamed the countryside, acting on tip-offs to recover abducted women? As Harini became common knowledge in the village by word of mouth, the squad swooped down on the little hut and carried her off, dazed and frightened. Nevertheless, she whispered to her rescuers about her sister Sita, who was located in all her finery.

"Who are you to take us away? Where are you taking us? I am all right here," Sita demanded suspiciously. Rescue operations were arbitrary. No woman could appeal against rescue. It was the honour of the men that was at stake. Sita sulked all the way to the camp. Then she imperiously demanded, "Send us home. They must be worried about us. You took long enough rescuing us."

But the old house had changed hands and no one knew where the family had fled. "They didn't wait for us?" Sita was incredulous and bitter, "Where will we go? You should have let us be there."

"Check in the camp records. Almost everyone is listed in it," she was told. Checking was a long and a tedious process and not always successful. The refugee camps were overcrowded, their staff overworked and harried, almost overcome by sheer numbers and human drama. And Harini was ill, drained and feverish. One day, the camp doctor said 'morning sickness', and suddenly Sita was all over her. "What have you done? What did you do? How did it happen?"

Harini looked at her dazed. "Do what?" she asked blankly.

"How did you get with child?"

"I am not a child." The childish innocence was still intact. The social workers intervened and sent Sita out of the tent. "Tell me everything – what happened to you? Who touched you? And your sister knew nothing?"

The child resurfaced. "Sita was busy with Shah. I played with the children and with Shahzada. He told us about Pinocchio and played with me, but it was painful only afterwards." Their mouths fell open. "Then he sent me to the *dhobi* who wanted to make me a *dhoban* and rear his *dhobi* son."

It was an impossible situation. Populations were in flux. Their family was untraceable. Sita acted *loco parentis* and took the decision for the abortion. It was discussed in whispers, "It is illegal. You'll have to go away from here. We'll give you the address of the doctor, Dr. Kapoor. You may have to wait, but don't leave it for too late…"

Harini knew nothing of the whole exercise, except pain and lassitude, traveling again in a truck with another crowd of people. "What will they do to me?"

Another city, another overcrowded camp and an overworked doctor, mopping his brow with a dirty handkerchief. "…Next."

Sita led her to the table. She spoke softly to the doctor and showed him their papers and the letter from the camp.

"How long are you going to mope like this, Harini? How long are we going to live here like beggars? Stitching *pajamas* and petticoats like *darzins* for ever. Get well so we can go and find the family," Sita urged her little sister. It was useless. Harini malingered. Sita's efforts to trace family came to a naught. One day she came across as a fellow lost soul suddenly walking purposefully.

"Where are you off to?"

"Haridwar."

"WHY?"

"That's the only way I know to trace my people. I know only one thing for certain, that some time or the other, some family member will die and the last rites will have to be performed at Haridwar. At that time, they will also visit the family Pandas to bring the family records up-to-date. That way I'll find out where they are and may be even meet some relative in Haridwar itself."

Sita jumped up. "We'll come with you. We've lost our people too. Maybe we too will make contact with our people." Sita was on a whirlwind. She held onto the hand of her new friend while she bustled about packing their few belongings. She harangued the camp officials into letting them go and badgered someone to write a letter of recommendation for accommodation at an *ashram* in Haridwar, wormed provisions for the journey out of the kitchen and some warm clothes against Haridwar's cold. "Harini is so sick, she needs these warm things, you know."

At Haridwar, Sita was doing all the reasonable efficient work. She met the *ashram* head and recounted their story, suitably edited, "Can you imagine what he would have said if I told him the whole truth…"

They were given a hot meal and then sent off to another *ashram* for women, with a large contingent of Sindhi women. "You'll feel more comfortable there, with your own people. Settle down and then contact your family *pandits* and leave a word with them," he advised her.

Sita was disconsolate. "Harini get well soon. How long are we going to live like this with only prayers and meditation all day? Cooking and cleaning? There's so much more to life!"

The younger girl, heartsick and physically drained, looked blankly at her sister.

"You wanted to come here. Now you don't have to stitch all day. We eat good food, say prayers, sing *bhajans*, live peacefully. What more do you want?"

"Don't you want to go home? Vadi Amma, the Dadas, Masis, Maamis, Chachis, our own sisters – don't you miss them all? Singing lovely songs, naughty, funny *laadas* at weddings, birthdays, and festivals? Don't you want to do all that? Get married? Wear lots of gold jewellery, diamonds, and beautiful embroidered silk and chiffon *saris*?"

Harini turned her face away. "I want nothing, just peace and no marriage. No man should even look at me, leave alone touch me," an involuntary shudder racked her whole body as she recalled everything that the camp workers had said about her when they thought she wasn't listening.

It was an unsettled situation. Sita wanted to leave the *ashram* at the earliest. Harini wouldn't think of it. Every now and then, Sita slipped away to the *pandits* who held the family genealogy, to check if anyone had come from home.

One day Sita ran into the members of another family, who had come to offer the last rites. She followed them through the rituals and then sat down with them, offering bits and pieces of her story and the family details.

"Please help me; my little sister is constantly ill. She needs mother's love. I want to take her home. If only there was some clue of where they could be. Please, please help us by telling our story to all your friends and relatives, maybe someone might know our people and write to us," she pleaded piteously, reeling off the names of the parents, uncles in different parts of the world, aunts, their in-laws, anyone to make a connection.

She even went to meet the *pandits* of other family groups to leave her family names, requesting them to forward the details through their *jajmans* (clients) when they came. At times she was totally despondent and despairing, "Why has no one come?"

Then she would come back frothing at the mouth, "Those pigs! Someone had come and they didn't tell them. They forgot us??"

But even the *pandit's* forgetting paid off. They got an address, Dada Vasudev's, never mind if it was a foreign one. Sita bought an air letter form and composed a piteous plea for rescue. "It'll take weeks to reach and then only can a reply come," warned her friends.

But Sita's impatience knew no bounds and a week later, she bought another air letter form and dashed off another letter. And then another, in vain.

No reply came. Several times, Sita went to check out the address. Once she met another person from the same place in Africa.

"You also live across the seven seas in Africa. You must know my brother Vasudev. Tell him when you go back that his sisters are waiting for him here in Haridwar," she entreated, giving them both Vasudev's address and her own along with a colorful description of their 'beggarly' situation.

Months later, a visitor came to the *ashram*. Sita was out. Harini was in meditation. The visitor was closeted with Guruji.

"Sita, someone has come to see you and Harini. Go to the office." She went on a winged feet and burst in. It just required one look at the narrow, baldhead, rimless-spectacled face for her to say, "Dada, Dada, you've come to rescue us".

She would have hugged him but he held her shoulders firmly at arm's length and examined her face carefully. Guruji tactfully left them alone.

"Dada, what took you so long?"

Sita would have launched off but Vasudev held up his hand peremptorily.

"You not only flooded me with letters, you sent messages with unknown people. Have you any idea what you were doing, embarrassing the family and me like that?"

Sita was stunned. Her mouth resembled a big 'O'.

"How would you have reached us otherwise? We didn't even know where you people were."

"So you have to broadcast it to the whole world that your family left you to the mercy of the *Mussalmans*? That you now wanted to come home after being despoiled by them?" THAT sounded ominous.

"What have we done? What were we to do?"

"You have lived, instead of dying of shame. That's what. Guruji tells me that Harini is just a little bit more than a vegetable. Instead of sitting quietly here and looking after her, you run around all the time, meeting all sorts of people and defaming your family. You want to come home? Which home? Whose home? You went away, we covered up that. Now people are forgetting the past. No one wants to rake it up and especially not you and Harini. How can I take you home to despoil the atmosphere there. There are so many other young girls to marry off and you both with the *Mussalmans*..." He shivered at the thought.

Sita was stunned. This scenario was totally unexpected.

"The family doesn't want us back? For no fault of our own? We didn't go, we were taken, held captive, beaten because the family didn't want that *Mussalmaani* Rajjo for Baba. How could a mother not want her living daughters back? Dada, you are our brother."

He put up his hand for silence. "I also have a wife and daughters. How will I let you into the household again after all that you've done? They still cry when they see Bharti."

"What have we done? Lived in a refugee camp and an *ashram* at Haridwar? Why? Because we were separated during the Partition. Dada, where is your sense of duty to family? To sisters? To the *rakhis* we used to tie on your wrist every year?"

Vasudev was unmoved. He stuck to his stand and called in his troops, Guruji and Guru Mata to pacify Sita, "*Beti*, he is not abandoning you. It is just that there is one daughter right there, lying in coma in the house since Partition. Already there are pointing fingers and whispers which have hampered many matches. For the sake of your family's good name, you must also sacrifice something. What you went through was your fate. But see, your bother is making provision for you both too."

Vasudev, it came out, had made a handsome donation to the *ashram*, with a promise of more to follow. It covered their expenses since they had come and for years to come.

"What do they need? Two meals, two white *saris*, a shawl, some soap and oil? How much does it come to? After all, they are my sisters."

That was Magnanimity personified. But Sita would have none of it.

"Are you finished?"

Eyes narrowed in her own inimitable style, she launched forth, "Now you listen to me. I will not live in this *ashram* anymore. You have two options. Either you get us a house where I can live like a human being instead of a white clad corpse, or I shall start travelling all over in a search of the family. There are just about half a dozen Sindhi clusters, okay, Delhi, Calcutta, Ajmer, Bhopal, Bombay, Poona, Bangalore, Madras. Somewhere someone will surface and if the family can't look after its own daughters, then it deserves what is coming when daughters will not hold back either. The choice is yours."

The brother and sister faced each other across the room. Guruji and Guru Mata looked on. It was the brother who blinked first, "Guruji says Harini wants to live here."

"You leave Harini to me. Have you even seen her yet?"

"How can you live alone? Here there are other people."

"You leave that to me."

"It'll be very expensive."

"Agreed. It would be cheaper to take us home."

"No!"

"Then?" Sita would have none of the arguments and Vasudev was cornered.

"Before you go from here, get me a house, furnish it and buy us proper clothes, provisions, furniture and leave money for other expenses. How much are you going to send every month? I am not a widow. I'll not live on nothing. Remember, I am Sita, your sister Sita," she warned Vasudev who was beginning to look worried.

Guru Mata added her own soft counsel. "It may be a good change to have your own house. But Sita, you may not be able to cope. Harini is not yet very strong; she will take a long time to be able to cope. You will have to bring her here when she is ill. She likes it here and is comfortable here. Maybe you could live close by and eat here?"

"Sometimes. Not always," Sita was sharp.

Finally, an agreement was hammered out. A small house was located, conveniently close to the *ashram*, the river and the *bazaar*. It was barely furnished.

"I want better beds, curtains and carpets. It is cold here," Sita declared firmly. "And clothes, coloured clothes."

"You can't wear those in the *ashram*," Vasudev remonstrated.

"I won't. I will wear them at home and in the *bazaar* and when we walk on the hills." Sita drove a hard bargain. Since Vasudev was no longer her Brother Dear, she had no compunction at all.

"I want us to live properly. And if you want our silence, you have to pay for it," she insisted firmly, listing expenses for furnishing the house according to their status, clothes, provisions for at least six months and dragging off Vasudev to open a bank account, which he was to replenish every month with a draft.

"Don't slip up," she warned. Besieged by the grabbing Sita, Vasudev totally ignored Harini, who only looked on mutely, her soft eyes pleading mutely for one loving look, one hug from her big brother. It was not to be.

Before he left, Vasudev called both sisters before Guruji. He placed their hands on each other's heads, "Swear that henceforth your lips will be sealed. You will tell no one who you are or your stories." Harini's eyes were clouded and sombre as she took her oath.

Vasudev left empty pocketed. He refused to part with any address, but promised a monthly dole to cover their expenses, leaving intact the major part of the donation to the *ashram*, so they would always be welcomed there when they wanted to go.

"Harini will come," Guru Mata had assured him.

But meanwhile, Sita had borne Harini away to their new little home, freshly whitewashed, a gay *dupatta* cut up into little curtains on the windows, brightly coloured covers on the bed and the table – colours with a vengeance as if to make up for the months of white. Harini winced. "White is so much more peaceful," she insisted.

"We are neither widows nor saints. White is good in summer, not all the time. Now we have to relearn living." Patiently, she took Harini back, to getting up to the sound of music other than *bhajans* – but where in Haridwar can one get away from the sound of the temple bells?

Sita took Harini for long walks, away from the river and its priests and beggars, to the hills, chasing butterflies and looking for birds and flowers, "See, Harini, look at those colourful butterflies. God made them too. Here today and gone tomorrow, but they will come back, just like the flowers. Nature regenerates itself. Things die out and then again flourish with a change of season. Why should we flout Nature? That was one phase of our life. Now God sent Dada and ordained the commencement of another phase. We must live it."

Harini liked to listen to Sita in such a philosophical mood. She missed the peace of the constant 'Om' chants in the *ashram*. Slowly, she was thawing to the sights and sounds that delighted Sita. Sometimes she did quietly visit the *ashram*, on her own.

One day, Sita came across her family *Panda*.

"When did you leave the *ashram*? Someone had come from your home."

She dragged him home to read the entries in his registers. There it was, Vadi Amma had died and two of her sons had come and more importantly, left the home address as Poona.

Sita was delirious. It was some time since they had been dependent on Vasudev who was resolute in not communicating at all. Only the draft to the bank every month, that's all. Sita had long given up on Harini, who was an apt pupil at the *ashram*. In a couple of decades, she would even become a Dadi (preacher) there. It was a hard found serenity, undaunted by her elder sister's growing rambunctiouness.

Sita collected friends, visitors and others around her, talked well into the night, read strange books and newspapers, even drank and smoked a *hookah* when she got a chance, at the homes of some of the rich *Marwaris*, whose wives and daughters she befriended. Now this lottery.

Tears welled up in both sisters' eyes, as they looked at the piece of paper with the address. Home, our home. They hugged and wept. Then they dried their eyes and composed a pleading letter.

The reply was prompt.

"Are you alive? Where? Why did you take so long to write? Why didn't you come home?"

The writer was Godu, short for Godavari, their elder sister, the Dadi of the Big House. She gave some tidbits of news and promised much more when she came to meet them as soon as the weather improved.

In the cool morning haze, white dotted the green of the vale under an azure sky. Morning prayers were underway when they arrived. As far as the eye could see, there were white *saris* all around, which made the pink all the more incongruous, set as it was in the *ashram* environment where there was an unspoken taboo on bright colours.

"Why only whites?" asked the young ones.

"It is not that all here are widows who must wear white only," it was explained, "But we want to avoid unnecessary complications."

"What complications? There's that lady in pink."

"Yes, she had been admonished. But she says it is *Karva Chauth* and she is fasting for the long life of her husband wherever he is. She feels that he must be alive, since he was in Eden when the Partition riots broke out. But she has lost touch with him and the rest of her family. So she lives here."

This run-up to Diwali was to have a special meaning for Sita and Harini that year. At long last, after how many uncounted years, they were with their own, Dadi, her daughter Mohini, Ammi and Sheel. They had come for the last rites of Baba and Bharti and to meet Sita and Harini.

There were many awkward moments, in catching up on the past. Both sisters were conscious of the solemn oath Vasudev had administered. "What should we tell them?" queried Harini anxiously.

"Nothing," said Sita firmly. "You remember nothing. You were in deep shock and very ill. All you can remember is camps, hospitals, and the *ashram* that is now your solace. I'll do all the talking."

Godu and Sita were chips of the same block; sparks were quicker to fly than the recounting of the family and personal histories. Godu's husband had come on leave, only to perish in the pre-Partition riots, the immediate cause of the family's panic stricken rush across the border.

"Where did you girls vanish suddenly? We scoured the city for you. How did you reach here?"

All eyes were taking in the contrast between the ravishing Sita in her glowing *salwar kurta* and net *dupatta* of the latest fashion and the subdued Harini clad in white as usual. "Why Haridwar? What happened to Harini?"

Sita fielded questions with aplomb. It was another matter altogether that she did not quite convince Godu of her heroics in bringing Harini across alive. But since the younger woman was silent and at the *ashram* they had been warned against pestering her, Sita's story was allowed to stand, that they were abducted and managed a lucky escape to travel with a *kafila* to Jalandhar and thence to Haridwar so that they might find some trace of the family through the *Pandas*.

Godu, hitherto the family's Partition Tragedy Queen, was not a little peaked at being out played by Sita. She mellowed when Sita resisted all her pleas to return home with them.

"How can we? How will we face so many people after so long? Dadi, see Harini hardly speaks to you all. What will happen at home when everyone piles on her? At least here, she can take refuge in the *ashram*. It gives her peace."

In vain did Dadi and the others coax. Sita was adamant, "We'll stay in touch. We'll be here whenever you come. But coming home will be difficult. You have just closed one painful chapter with Bharti and Baba. Why open another?"

Dadi felt a bitter undertone when Sita mentioned Baba. The thought was fleeting and she did not think it wise to probe. It was obvious that the older women loathed to leave Sita and Harini in Haridwar. They even appealed to Guruji at the *ashram*. But he advised them to leave the girls to slowly heal their own wounds.

"Who knows they may one day pay you a visit. Stay in touch with them, but don't use any force, especially for Harini's sake," he warned. "Don't talk about them at home to, too many people," he said conscious of his patron, Vasudev's reservations.

Dadi, who earlier looked askance at Sita, now became very generous. Before she left, she took off her gold bangles and Mohini's and gave them to Sita and Harini. And ever after, she sent parcels of presents, pretty *saris*, perfumes and trinkets selected from the bags that came from all corners of the world with brothers returning from abroad.

As the resident daughter, Dadi ran the Big House from the money sent home by all the brothers. She also fulfilled all the family's social and other obligations and invested in the real estate etc.

It was her privilege not only to discuss finances and accounts with the brothers, but also to open the trunks they came laden with and to supervise the distribution of the booty from the foreign lands. The opening of the trunks was a family tradition that Dadi clung on to. Perhaps it was her insecurity over having no husband or a family of her own. But she clung to her maiden privilege, inviting the ire of her bhabhis who dared not remonstrate that it should be their privilege to open their own husbands' bags. "You have got me, why do you need the trunk?" Vasudev had remonstrated once with his wife. That settled the matter forever more for every one.

But it was at such times that being the distributor of the largesse won Dadi more ill-will than gratitude. For her partialities were obvious and rancour often ran deep between her and the respective bhabhis as well as the recipients of the gifts, which ranged from innocuous Cutex nail polishes, lipsticks, baubles of costume jewellery, musical albums and cigarette lighters to opulent silks and even fancy dragon-designed dinner services.

Shortly after Dadi's visit, Sita fell ill. She contracted TB and Harini was hard put to look after her. Guru Mata had reservations about Harini's own health. For all her vitality, Sita had a very quick succumb to Death. It was as if she had only been waiting to reconcile with the family before she went.

A dry-eyed Harini sat with her at the end and then supervised the last rites.

"Sita is gone and I am all alone now," she thought. Another thought drifted in, "Vasudev Dada's *kasam* is gone with Sita." But she held her peace. After selling the house and Sita's pictures and jewels, Harini took sanctuary in the *ashram*, knowing no one would dare to take her away from there.

"I can cope with family for a couple of days three to four times a year," she confided, "not all the time."

Thus, Harini metamorphosed into Dadi Hari. The family had its own resident guru.

*****